BEWARE
OF *Me*

New York Times and *USA Today* Bestselling Author

CYNTHIA
EDEN

Copy-editing by: J. R. T. Editing

PROLOGUE

Carly Shay heaved against the ropes that held her prisoner. The rough hemp cut into her wrists, making her bleed even more and the wooden chair that she was tied to shuddered as she jerked and twisted. Her hair fell into her face as she screamed, "Don't! Stop!" Tears streaked down her cheeks. "Please, I am begging you, don't hurt him anymore!"

But the men kept up their attack. Not on her, not now. She wasn't the target right then.

Ethan was.

Ethan Barclay. The man who'd been her only friend on most days—and the man she'd secretly loved for the last two years.

But Ethan was on the floor, and four of Quincy's goons—Quincy Atkins, a man who truly had to be the devil—were beating him.

Was Ethan still moving? Still alive?

"Please!" Her cry was both a plea and a scream. "Stop hurting him!"

Quincy stepped forward. A big, hulking man. *He hurt me.* So much. But...she slammed the door on that thought. She couldn't go there, not right then. She couldn't remember all that he'd taken from her. The memories would come later, she knew that.

Right then...she just had to help Ethan. He'd come to save her, but if she didn't do something, soon, he'd be the one to wind up dying.

Quincy Atkins was a crime boss who pretty much ran D.C. Terrifying. Psychotic. And he wanted her.

What Quincy wanted, he took.

Don't remember. Don't. Focus on Ethan.

Because Ethan's golden eyes had just met hers. She could see that he was gathering his strength. Preparing for an attack.

Ethan. Twenty-one years old. A fixture on the D.C. streets. He'd always watched her back. Always looked out for her. She knew the whispers—the stories that said Ethan was turning into just as much of a criminal as Quincy. That Ethan was even *gunning* for Quincy but...

Those stories were wrong. Ethan was good. He was her friend. He'd risked his life for her. She didn't care what anyone else thought of him.

Ethan is good...

But if she didn't stop Quincy, Ethan would be a dead man.

As she watched, Quincy motioned for his men to leave the room. Relief made her a little dizzy. *Maybe he'll stop now. Maybe...*

But as soon as the others were gone, Quincy took a knife from the sheath at his hip. 'I'm gonna cut Loverboy open," Quincy announced, his voice cold and cruel. "Then you'll be mine. Body and soul. I'll own every inch of you...and *no one* will ever be able to help you again."

This was her fault. All her fault. She'd taken the job dancing at his club. She'd lied about her age to get the gig, but she'd needed the money so desperately—her dad, he wasn't well. If she hadn't gotten that money, she and her dad would have been cast out on the street.

Her gaze slid back to Ethan. His handsome face was battered, but his golden eyes glittered. He wouldn't stop fighting. Giving up wasn't in his blood. He'd battle Quincy and Quincy's men until—*until Ethan died.*

Then what would she do? Her hands kept jerking at the ropes behind her. Her whole body hurt. She had so many bruises. So much pain. But she wouldn't let Quincy take Ethan away from her. Almost distantly, she heard herself say... "Please. Don't hurt him anymore. Don't. I'll do anything—just *don't!*"

But even before those words were fully out of her mouth, Quincy had lunged toward Ethan. As she yanked against her ropes, Quincy kicked Ethan in the ribs, again and again. Then Quincy rolled Ethan onto his back and put the knife right over Ethan's heart.

This can't happen! I won't let it!

Her fear faded as rage burned through her. Quincy had taken too much from her already. He wasn't going to take Ethan, too.

Quincy's back was to her. And in that moment, as she saw him with that knife over Ethan's heart, something broke inside of Carly—even as the ropes that bound her finally gave way. Carly shot out of the chair and lunged for Quincy. "Don't hurt him!" It wasn't a plea this time. Her words were a roar.

She slammed into Quincy's back. They both fell down, tangling over Ethan's body. She heard Quincy give a choked gasp and she scrambled back as he heaved up—

Only to immediately sag back to the ground.

That was when she saw that the knife wasn't in Ethan's chest. When she'd slammed into Quincy, she *had* saved Ethan. She started to smile and then she saw—

The knife is in Quincy's chest. She hadn't meant to stab him, had she? No, no, she'd just wanted to stop him and he'd fell—gotten all tangled up and somehow the knife had gone into him. The handle stuck out, but at least half of the blade was in his chest. In his heart?

Quincy opened his mouth, and she realized that the guards were just outside of that door. If they heard their boss call for them, if they rushed in and saw what she'd done...

I'm dead. Ethan's dead.

Carly put her hand over Quincy's mouth. The tears kept pouring from her eyes. Shudders racked her body. She could feel Quincy's lips moving beneath her palm. Nausea rolled in her stomach, and Carly thought she might vomit.

Ethan crawled toward her. He left a trail of blood in his path. His hand lifted—

Ethan?

And he shoved the knife even deeper into Quincy's chest. Quincy's lips stopped moving beneath her palm.

She kept her hand over his mouth. She couldn't move. Couldn't hear anything but the scream—a scream echoing only in her mind.

She'd done this. She'd killed a man. Killed the man who'd attacked her, raped her, who'd tried to kill Ethan.

And now...now his men were just outside the door. She wasn't going to get away. There would never be an escape for her.

Ethan's fingers curled around her wrist. "It's okay, baby," he told her, his voice a rough rasp.

No, it was so far from *okay* that it wasn't even funny, but Carly couldn't manage to speak.

"I'm...going to take care of everything," Ethan said, his words little more than a whisper. "All you have to do...is trust me."

His hand lifted—the hand that had just driven that knife deeper into Quincy's chest, and his fingers curled around her wrist. Slowly, he moved her hand away from Quincy's mouth.

I did that. I killed him.

For Ethan, for her own survival...*I'd do it again.*

Darkness stretched inside of her, threatening to consume her. She clamped her lips together to hold back the scream that wanted to break free.

"Trust me," Ethan said again.

But she was afraid she'd never trust anyone again.

Especially...not herself.

CHAPTER ONE

Present Day...

Carly Shay hurried up the subway steps, her high heels making the climb feel far more difficult than it should. People jostled around her, moving quickly, but she kept pace with them. After all, she'd been living in New York for years. She knew this town. Knew this place inside and out.

The crowds—the wonderful energy—she could disappear in this city. Blend in easily. And no one gave her a second glance.

That was why she'd first come to New York. To vanish in the crowd. To stop attracting attention. The way Carly figured it, she'd done a damn good job of vanishing.

One hand kept a firm grip on her bag as she marched forward and across the street. A few more minutes, and she'd be home free.

"Carly."

She almost slammed into him. She'd been focused on the crowd. On the guy in the fancy suit who was yelling into his phone. On the mother trying to comfort her crying toddler.

She hadn't even seen *him*.

But now, she couldn't look anywhere else.

Because in the middle of the sidewalk, standing less than three feet from her, was the man who haunted far too many of her dreams. Well, her nightmares really.

Ethan Barclay.

Tall, dark, and far too dangerous to know...Ethan Barclay.

The dying sunlight fell on his dark hair. Hair that was a little too long. Dark stubble covered his jaw and his golden eyes—tiger eyes—were locked on her with the full intensity of a predator who'd just found the perfect prey.

I won't be his prey. Not this time.

"You left D.C. without saying good-bye," Ethan told her. His hands were shoved deeply into the pockets of his coat, and that coat stretched across his broad shoulders. *Powerful.* Yes, she knew Ethan was incredibly strong. He wasn't the twenty-one-year-old boy she'd known so long ago.

He was a man now. A stranger. One who was reputed to be far more dangerous than Quincy Atkins had ever been.

When Quincy vanished, Ethan took over D.C. And...

Carly had tried to pick up the pieces of her life.

Even though it was warm for New York at that time of the year, a shiver slid over Carly. "I...I was only back in D.C. to check on my step-sister."

"Um..." His voice was a low, deep rumble and he was closing in on her. Eliminating that space between them as he stalked closer. Someone jostled her from behind, but before Carly could stumble, Ethan's hands—big, strong, but oddly gentle as they held her—curled around her shoulders. "Back in D.C. long enough to save Julianna's life...and get shot."

She'd been shot twice, actually. But it had been worth it. Julianna had been put at risk because she'd been trying to protect Carly—and the crimes from Carly's past. *Quincy's murder.* "I wasn't going to let Julianna be hurt again because of me."

His eyelashes flickered. Long eyelashes. They should have looked ridiculous on a man like him, but they didn't. They just made his intense eyes appear all the...sexier. Dammit. She shouldn't find him sexy. Not at all. She should have moved way, way beyond him by this point.

The way he'd moved beyond her.

"I thought you were going to die." His voice was rough as he made that confession. Ragged around the edges. Very much *not* Ethan.

You don't know him any longer. You probably never knew him—not the real guy.

"You were bleeding out on the floor of that apartment," Ethan said, as his hold tightened on her. "And during the ambulance ride to the hospital, shit, you left me."

She stilled. "I didn't know you were in the ambulance with me." *And I left him? What does that mean?* No one had said anything about her paying some visit to the afterlife. Maybe the EMTs didn't share that info with her though because they might have realized...*it freaks me out.*

"I was in the ambulance," he told her grimly. "And at your hospital bedside, until I realized that I was a threat to you."

Carly had to swallow to ease the growing lump in her throat. *You're always a threat to me.*

"But I left too late, and now others know..."

"Okay, Ethan, I really don't get why you're in New York, but we don't have anything to discuss." Did her voice sound cool? Dismissive? Probably not, but she'd really been aiming for that tone. "Now let me go because I want to get home." It had been her first day back at her job since she'd been shot and she was exhausted. It took all of her strength not to show that weakness to him, but she knew that if he realized how close to trembling she was...the guy would pounce.

"You know why I'm in New York." He didn't let her go. In fact, he seemed to inch even closer. Because Ethan was a big guy, well over six feet, she had to tip back her head as she gazed up at him. Even in heels, she didn't come close to his height. "I'm here for you."

Once, she'd longed to hear him say those words. When she'd been a terrified teenager, when she hadn't been able to deal with the guilt and shame and horror of what had happened to her...she'd longed for him. She'd broken, her whole world imploding when her father had passed away so closely behind her attack by Quincy.

And a psych ward had become her home when she'd lost control.

I screamed for Ethan. But Ethan hadn't been there. "Let's be clear on a few things." She kept her body stiff in his hold. "Our relationship is over. Long over." As in...*years* over. "It ended one blood-soaked night when you put me in a cab and just walked away from me. You didn't contact me again...you didn't so much as call me. You built up your life and you moved the hell on." Now she jerked back, tearing out of his hands because she didn't want his touch. It made her remember too much about the past. "And now, so have I. Just because I returned to D.C. to help my *sister,* that did not mean that I went back for you."

His eyes glittered with emotion.

"Now get out of my way, Ethan. Because we're done."

His blazing stare raked over her. "How many secrets do you carry?"

She wasn't going to keep talking to him in the middle of that crowded street. In fact, she wasn't going to keep talking to him at all. She had a life now. A good life. She wasn't going to throw it away. Her past—and the secrets there—were locked up tightly inside of her. Carly took a deep breath, and she gave Ethan a wide berth as she headed around him. If he wouldn't move, she'd just keep going on her own.

Keep going...*and keep in control.* Carly knew maintaining control of her emotions was vital. She'd contained her pain and anger for years. Nothing got past her control these days.

But then she heard his footsteps, and Carly realized that Ethan was following her.

No, no, no.

"I let you go once before..." His words drifted to her. "Do you have any fucking idea just how hard that was for me?"

Impossible. "You sent me away." She kept walking.

"Because I'd already brought you blood and death and hell."

No, she'd done that...herself.

"I can't do it again," Ethan said. "I won't..."

The crosswalk light up ahead was red. She had to stop at the corner. He closed in behind her, and she could actually feel the warmth of his body reaching out to her and then—his fingers brushed along her hip. Her eyes closed, just for a moment, as her control cracked, faint spider-webs of emotion breaking through the surface.

Then she made her eyes open.

"I want something for myself," Ethan said. "I want you."

Liar, liar. "You've got plenty of women, Ethan. Go back to D.C. Go back to them." The crosswalk light changed. Green. Yes! "Leave me the hell alone."

"Sorry, baby," his voice murmured after her. "But that just isn't going to be possible."

Her steps quickened. She didn't look back at him. Ethan had left her alone for years. No visits, no notes, nothing. Now he suddenly wanted back in her life? Like she was supposed to believe he'd missed her or some crazy crap like that?

No, she wasn't a fool. She also wasn't looking back. Because she didn't want to see if he was following her or not. She didn't care.

Really.

Dammit.

She kept walking, heading toward her building. It was a brownstone—one that her company actually owned. She'd been allowed to take one of the apartment's there as part of one very sweet employment deal. Some days, Carly still couldn't believe her luck on that one. But she wasn't going to question fate too much. After all the hard times she'd had, a little bit of good luck had been ever-so-welcome.

A few minutes later, she could see the hard, heavy lines of the building. Old architecture on the outside, but the place had been completely updated on the inside. She'd be home free soon, locked inside her home. No way would Ethan get to her then.

If he's still following me.

Maybe she should spare a glance over her shoulder. Just in case. Just to be sure—

"Ms. Shay?"

A man in a fancy suit had straightened as she approached. Handsome, with close-cropped dark hair and blue eyes. He flashed her a quick smile even as he approached her.

Okay, now what?

"Ms. Shay, I need a moment of your time."

The guy had better not be some kind of salesman. "I'm sorry," she said, voice apologetic, "but I've had a really long day and—"

"Your wounds have probably sapped your strength," he cut in, nodding. "No doubt, you just want to go inside and collapse after your first day back on the job."

Goosebumps rose on her arms.

"But I can't let you collapse just yet." His smile hardened a bit. "Like I said, I need a moment of your time."

She backed up a step. And suddenly, the idea that Ethan might be trailing her—that idea wasn't so scary. *The devil you know...*

Is far better than the one you don't.

"Who are you?" Carly asked him, notching up her chin.

He pulled a wallet out of his pocket. No, not a wallet—ID. Real official looking ID. "I'm with the FBI, ma'am. My name is Special Agent Victor Monroe, and I need to talk with you about Quincy Atkins."

No, no, no. Her heart stopped beating. She stared up at the special agent and actually felt her world start to collapse around her. This couldn't be happening. He couldn't *know* what she'd done. Could he?

Victor Monroe's head tilted to the right. "Are you okay, Ms. Shay? You've gone quite pale."

"I-I'm still recovering, like you said." She put her hand to her temple. "And it's warm today. I-I need to get inside and cool down. Our talk will have to wait..."

But when she tried to step around him, the FBI agent—Victor—moved into her path. "It can't wait." Suspicion had sharpened his gaze. "Can't help but notice...you don't act at all surprised to hear that a federal agent wants to question you about a missing crime lord."

Her heart was racing now—seeming to shake her chest. And her mouth had gone bone-dry.

"Do you know where Quincy Atkins is, Ms. Shay?"

Hell. That was exactly where she suspected he was. But she wasn't about to tell the FBI special agent that fact. "How would I know? I think I saw some special on *20/20* about him. The man's been missing for years."

His hand reached out and curled around her shoulder. At that touch, Carly flinched. It was her normal reaction to being touched. Only...*I didn't flinch when Ethan touched me.* She'd figure out that messed up thought later, but for the moment... "I want you to take your hand off me." Her voice was cool. "I don't know anything about Quincy Atkins and his disappearance, so I don't have anything to say to you."

Victor's jaw hardened as his hand immediately dropped. "I'm here to help you."

"I doubt that." Carly wondered how he'd even learned about her...and her connection to Quincy. Someone had tipped off the FBI, obviously, but just who was that someone? She marched briskly for her building.

"I have reason to believe that you may be connected to Quincy's disappearance." The agent was shadowing her steps. Making her way too nervous. "And if I have reason to believe that..." He sighed. "Then others will believe it, too. You may find yourself...hunted."

At that one word, *hunted,* Carly turned to face him. "Are you trying to frighten me?" She thought he was.

He didn't deny her accusation. Instead, Victor said, "When you were seventeen years old, you were put in a psych ward for three weeks. That was two weeks *after* Quincy Atkins vanished. That timeline is interesting, don't you think? Especially since I know you worked as a dancer at Quincy's club, and word from some of the people who knew him back then, well, they said Quincy took a special interest in you."

"A special interest," she repeated, disgust sharp in her voice, "in a seventeen year old girl."

He stepped even closer to her. She didn't like it. Fear rose within her. Because this agent—he could destroy her life. She knew it. He was staring at her with speculation in his eyes, and the guy could probably smell the blood trail that led straight to her.

"I can be an enemy," Victor told her. "Or I can be a friend. It all depends on you."

She shook her head. "What are you asking? For me to make some kind of deal with you?"

"You don't strike me as the killing type," Victor told her.

Then you don't know me very well.

"But if you know who *did* kill Quincy Atkins, if you know what happened...your life could be in danger. I can help you. The FBI can protect you. We can—"

"You can move the hell away from her, asshole."

Carly's breath heaved out at that low, deadly command. A command that had come from Ethan. Her gaze shot to the left, and he was there, glaring at the FBI agent and his golden gaze seemed to burn with fury.

Two things were clear to her in that moment. One, Ethan *had* kept following her. So that meant he'd probably been close and overheard her whole conversation with the FBI guy.

And two, the FBI agent—he didn't look surprised at all to see Ethan standing a few feet away. In fact, Victor turned to look at Ethan and said, "And the predators are already closing in...See, Ms. Shay, I told you that you'd be hunted."

Ethan smiled, a chilling sight. "I don't think we've had the pleasure of a formal introduction, and I don't really fucking want one. What I want is for you to step away from my fiancée."

His what now?

"And I want you to go back to whatever government hole you crawled out of. Carly doesn't concern you, and you need to stay away from her."

She could practically feel the tension rolling off the agent. His gaze cut to her, and the smile he gave her was obviously forced. "You're going to need a friend soon." Victor handed her a card and forced her fingers to curl around it. "When you realize just how much danger you're in, call me." Then he leaned in toward her and said, "Because the *last* thing that you want to do...that's trust him. Ethan Barclay is a threat to you, and if you're as smart as I've been led to believe, you'll realize that. And you'll come to me as fast as you can."

"She doesn't like it when strangers touch her." Ethan was just a step away now. "So either get your hand off her, or I *will* be removing it."

The agent's hand slid away from hers. He nodded to Carly and said, "I hope I hear from you soon." Then he was gone. Heading down the street with a confident, determined stride.

She still held his card in her hand. And Ethan— "Fiancée?" she murmured.

"It sounded good to me."

It sounded terrifying to her.

"Let's go inside, baby," he told her gruffly. "Because we have seriously got to talk."

The last thing you want to do...that's trust him. Oh, hell.

***

She was afraid of him. Not surprising, really. Ethan knew that most people were afraid of him, and with good reason. He didn't make for a good enemy. In fact, becoming his enemy was usually a fatal mistake.

Carly's hands were shaking as she shut her door and secured the lock. He was inside, she'd let him in without another argument, and his gaze slid around her home. It was odd. He knew Carly had been living there for about six months, but there weren't a lot of personal touches in the place. It still had that "decorator" look, as if Carly didn't want to change anything that had been there before.

Carly had once loved bright colors. Bold art. She'd laughed freely and danced—

He cut off that thought. Hard. Because he'd once seen her dance when he should *not* have seen that show. When no one should have seen it.

"The FBI knows that I—"

He lunged toward her and in one, fast move, he had his hand over her mouth. Her soft lips pressed against his palm even as her blue eyes flared wide with fear. *I hate for her to fear me.* Fear was good, as long as that fear came from anyone but her. Ethan brought his mouth close to her right ear and whispered, "The FBI was waiting outside of your building. I don't trust those guys." Not when he knew how badly they wanted to nail his ass to the wall. "There could be a listening device in here." The whole place could be wired. So the last thing he wanted her to do..."*No confessions, baby,*" Ethan ordered, his voice a bare breath of sound.

She gave a slow nod.

His hand fell from her lips. Her scent—sweet and sexy and all Carly—wrapped around him. He knew he should step back, but he didn't. He kept her pinned there, trapped between his body and the door, and Ethan thought about all the mistakes he'd made in his life.

The biggest one? Letting her go.

I won't do that again.

"You should pack a bag and come with me. I have a suite in town. We can talk there." Talk, fuck, whatever she wanted.

She wasn't seventeen anymore.

Two consenting adults—and he'd never wanted anyone more than he wanted her.

"I'm not going anywhere with you," Carly said.

Pity. But he hadn't expected things with her to be easy. He had a whole lot of ground to make up.

"That agent—Victor—he just said I was being hunted—why? Why would anyone want to hunt me? How does anyone even know about my connection to Quincy?"

She wasn't getting the whole listening device bit. Sighing, Ethan caught her wrist in his hand and he said, "Come with me."

Then he pulled her down the hallway and opened the door on the right. He headed into her bathroom and shut the door behind them.

"What are you doing?" Now her voice had cracked a bit. "Why are we in the bathroom? How did you even know this *was* my bathroom?"

Because I own the building. I also own the company you work for, baby. But he didn't tell her that, not yet.

He was coming across stalkerish enough without that big reveal.

"You'd better not start stripping," Carly told him, voice sharp. "'Cause I don't know what you think is happening here, but—"

He put a finger over her lips. She blinked up at him.

Sadly, no stripping will happen.

When she fell into silence, he reached for the faucet. He cranked the water on and let it run full-blast into the shower. For a moment, he stared at that rushing water. Oh, but he could imagine stripping and being naked in that shower with Carly. The water would pour over her skin and he'd lick every single inch of her.

"Ethan! Seriously, what the hell are you doing?"

He shook his head and temporarily said goodbye to that fantasy. "I'm giving us some sound cover. If there are listening devices, they won't hear us, not over the shower." But he had to get in real close while he talked to her. She'd pressed her back against the door, and he put his hand up against the wood, leaning in toward to her. He hated the way she tensed when he was near. It was like she sensed just how close he truly was to jumping her.

"Oh...so we're not here for...*oh*."

His brows rose. "If you want to strip with me, hell, yes, I'm game."

Her lips pressed together.

"I'm always game for you," he added, just so there would be no doubt on that point.

He saw the small movement of her throat as she swallowed. Her lashes lowered, concealing her gaze. "You forgot me for years. Now you're back. An FBI agent is on my doorstep and—"

He caught her chin in his left hand. "Look at me."

Her lashes lifted.

"Many things happened over the years, but forgetting you? That wasn't one of them. I *never* forgot you." She didn't get it, and probably never would. When he'd watched her walk out of his life—that had been the hardest thing he'd ever done. Because he'd already seen the danger in her...he'd known that Carly Shay could wreck him. Could own him.

And he'd known that he would break any law to have her.

Seventeen.

Hell, yes, he'd had to send her away. She'd deserved a life. A good one.

Not some criminal bastard like him.

Then she came back. And all hell has broken loose.

"You don't need to lie to me," Carly snapped. "You've had so many lovers—I barely registered on your radar. I didn't even—"

Now she was pissing him off. So he leaned in even closer. "Yeah, I've had lovers. Plenty of them. And you know what? They weren't *you*. You think I didn't try like hell to get you out of my system? The shit I feel for you isn't healthy or safe, but it's there, and it's consumed me for years. So don't tell me that I forgot you." He shook his head. "Never have, never would."

For an instant, he could have sworn that pain flickered in her gaze, and his own chest burned then because the *last* thing he ever wanted was to hurt her. He knew she deserved someone a hell of a lot better than him, and he'd tried to play the noble card, even though that wasn't his style. But she'd...hell, she'd *killed* to keep him safe. When someone did that, you owed the woman.

More than can be repaid.

But he was trying, dammit.

"Daniel Duvato." Just saying the name pissed him off. "Remember my psycho ex-bodyguard?" Actually, the guy had been his friend—fucking family. And he'd been a cold-blooded killer. Daniel had gone after anyone that he thought Ethan had cared about. *So it's a good thing I made sure you were far away from me. Because he would have killed you, and I would have gone insane.* "When he was arrested, he wanted to make a deal with the cops. He was spouting BS and talking to anyone who would listen." He heaved out a long sigh. "And one of the things he was talking about so freaking much? You, me, and Quincy Atkins." He paused and had to say, "You know he had a video of that crime."

She paled. "A video you destroyed."

Yes, he had. Once he'd found out about the damn thing. By that point, the damage had been done. *Daniel, I hope you are roasting in hell right now.* He'd trusted the guy, and all along, Daniel had wanted to destroy him.

Daniel had said that he'd helped clean up the Quincy crime scene. Instead, he'd taken the security footage and kept it, waiting for the perfect moment to use that in his war against Ethan.

The war is over, asshole. You're dead. I'm still alive.

"You...you *did* destroy the video, right, Ethan?" Her voice shook.

"Yeah, baby, I did." But he had to be honest with her. "I found out that Daniel got word to the FBI. He wanted to talk to them about Quincy's disappearance. Lucky for us, Daniel is dead now."

Not even by Ethan's hands. "So he can't tell the FBI anything else, but he sure made folks curious about what he knew."

Like the FBI jerk who'd been outside. That guy had sure closed in fast. As soon as Ethan had learned of the FBI's new interest in Quincy Atkins, he'd started working to get a new safe place set up for Carly.

"Maybe I should tell the FBI agent the truth," she said.

What? Ethan shook his head, sure that he'd misheard her.

"I won't talk about you." Her shoulders sagged a bit. "I'll confess that Quincy kidnapped me. I got loose. We fought. And the knife—it went into his chest."

She was still trying to protect him. After all those years? How could he *not* be insane for her? "No. That's not going to happen. The FBI isn't dragging you down."

"But—"

"I'll handle the FBI. And you..." Damn but it was so hard to be this close to her and not kiss her. Her lips were right there. Inches from his. Full and plump and perfect. But when he kissed her, he pretty much ignited.

Beautiful Carly. She'd grown to be even more gorgeous over the years. Her wild child look was gone...no more short shorts and loose t-shirts. Now she was all sleek elegance. Perfectly cut clothes—a fancy blouse made of silk and a pencil skirt that fell just above her knees. Her hair—now shot with red highlights—was pulled back in a slick ponytail, and that style just accentuated her almond-shaped eyes. Big, dark blue eyes. A faint sprinkling of freckles slid across her nose, and he found that little sprinkle freaking delectable.

"What about me?" Carly demanded.

She wasn't going to like this part. "I think you should start packing." He'd originally hoped to follow her to New York and do something incredibly normal...like ask the woman out on a date. But with the FBI closing in, hell, no, that wasn't a good sign. The FBI would come first, and other—more undesirable bastards—would follow in their wake. There were plenty of people out there who would like to know what had happened to Quincy Atkins, and those people wouldn't hesitate to hurt Carly in order to discover the truth.

Ethan had no intention of allowing her to be hurt. He didn't want her skin so much as fucking bruised.

"Packing?" She blinked at him, then gave a ragged laugh. "You're crazy."

"Perhaps. Probably." He shrugged, not overly concerned with that bit. "But I'm still going to need you to get your bag ready. Everything you want to take with you. Feel free to leave unnecessary shit behind. I'll buy you new stuff and you can—"

"No." Her hands came up and shoved against his chest. He took a step back, mostly because he'd been caught off-guard by the force of her shove. "I'm not leaving," Carly said adamantly. "Forget that. I have a life here."

"A life that could end if you aren't careful." A life that would be destroyed if she talked to the FBI.

Her chin notched up. "Maybe I'm tired of running from the past."

"Too bad. Because the past isn't dead. You aren't safe, and that's on me. I'm the one who attracted attention to you when I wouldn't leave your bedside. I'm the one who put you in the crosshairs, so now I'm the one who will keep you safe."

She licked her lips. Rather helplessly, his gaze followed that sensual movement and—

"Get out, Ethan."

He shook his head.

"Out," Carly enunciated slowly. "Out of my home. Out of my life. You aren't doing this to me. You aren't going to appear and—and take me away. This isn't happening."

Yes, it was. He'd wanted to ease her into the situation, but the FBI had moved too fast.

"I like things here. I'm safe." She heaved out a hard sigh. "I need that safety. Being with you—*you aren't safe, Ethan.*"

No, he wasn't.

"I need to think, so I want you gone."

"We both need to go," he said, fighting to keep the emotion from his voice. He didn't want to force her to leave, didn't want to reveal just how much he'd already been in her life, but...*I can't risk her.*

"I'm not leaving. I-I can't." She slid a hand over her face, and he noticed the tremble in her fingers. Hell, she *was* still recovering from the gunshots. She needed to be sleeping right then, not dealing with this mess. "I want you to walk away from me, Ethan. Just like you did before. If the FBI comes at me, I'll—"

"Don't tell them the truth." Because that would be another nightmare.

Her hand fell. "I'll handle them, and I won't incriminate you, okay? If that's what you're so worried about, just relax."

"I'm worried about you." Why couldn't she see that?

She slid around him, no longer meeting his stare, and she turned off the storm of water. "Leave now, Ethan."

Hell. "This is a huge mistake."

"Then it's my mistake to make."

He didn't move. He couldn't. "You're going to need me."

"I haven't needed you in years."

At those words, he flinched.

"You have a way of wrecking my world, Ethan," she said softly. "I don't want that anymore."

Every muscle in his body had turned to stone. "You mean...you don't want me."

She didn't speak.

Fuck. He'd waited too long with her. But sometimes, you didn't realize just what the hell you had...until you saw her bleeding out in the back of an ambulance. *I can't lose her.* "When you get scared," his voice was gruff, "when you think the world is going to pieces around you, I'll be there. I can help you. I *will* help you."

Her solemn gaze finally rose to meet his.

"Don't forget that." And, because he couldn't help it, because he had to taste her before he walked away, Ethan closed the distance between them. His head lowered toward her, the movement slow, giving her the chance to back away.

She didn't. Her hands rose to his chest once more. Would she push him away? Shove him again?

She didn't.

"Ethan..." There was desire in her voice. A need. He understood—they both felt that physical connection, one that nothing could ever seem to sever. "You are so wrong for me," she said.

And she was the only right thing in his world.

His lips brushed over hers. Slowly. Carefully. He savored her. Tasted her just enough...just enough to make him want so much more.

Then her mouth parted. Her tongue slid out and licked against his lower lip. That sensual touch went straight through his body, and his cock—already eager for her—jerked up even more. He took the kiss deeper. Made it harder as he tasted her—as he thrust his tongue into her mouth and thought of all the things he wanted to do with her.

To her.

If he'd been a better man, he never would have gone back into her life.

But...fuck that. Screw being good.

Ethan's head lifted. "I'll be close, when you need me."

Then, before he could change his mind, before he could give in to the temptation to strip her right there, Ethan turned and walked away. He kept walking, until he was outside of her place. He paused on the front steps, glaring into the approaching night, his hands clenched at his sides.

It was easy enough to see the non-descript van parked at the curb. The FBI—so predictable. They'd be watching Carly for the night. So she'd be safe enough.

He'd give her this night. Long enough to realize that she needed him.

Then he'd have to take her away from the life she'd built. Because there was no choice. Not for either of them.

***

He wasn't the first one to find the target. Watching from the shadows, he saw Ethan Barclay stalk out of the building, anger evident in every line of his body as he paused to glare at the van on the corner.

FBI agents were in that van.

Well, well...so the gossip he'd learned had been true. The woman called Carly Shay was an important piece in the puzzle—the puzzle that was the disappearance of Quincy Atkins.

He'd been trying to solve that mystery for years. A man like Quincy didn't just vanish, not without plenty of help.

As Ethan marched away, he settled back into the shadows. He knew the right time to approach his prey. And he also knew the right time to wait.

The FBI wouldn't be around forever. Carly Shay wouldn't always have a guard. The minute she was vulnerable...

Then it will be my turn for a little one-on-one time with Carly...

CHAPTER TWO

Carly hadn't packed a bag. She also hadn't slept much, either, but the next morning, she was dressed and ready for work and she hurried out of her building with the intention of getting her life absolutely back to normal.

She wasn't going to run. She wasn't going to let Ethan scare her.

She also had decided—around two a.m.—that a big reveal to the FBI probably wasn't in her best interest, either. *I don't want to spend the rest of my life in jail.* Not for the death of a murdering, raping bastard like Quincy Atkins.

Her heels clicked over the pavement. There was a cable company van parked a block away and she glanced over at it quickly. Maybe they'd finally get her service back up and running. Maybe—

Her phone rang.

Pausing just a moment, Carly pulled it out of her purse and glanced at the screen. When she saw the number there, Carly couldn't help but tense. She'd been avoiding this particular call for a reason.

She started to ignore the ring but...

Deal with it. Deal with him. Her finger slid across the screen and she lifted the phone to her ear. "Hello."

"Carly?" The voice was smooth and deep, easily recognizable even though the caller then said, "This is Dr. Nelson. I've been worried about you."

Right. Because he was the worrying type.

"You missed your last appointment..."

That would be due to the fact that she'd been in the hospital, unconscious. But she didn't tell him that. He'd probably freak out. "Sorry about that," she said, quickening her pace even as she glanced around her. Because of Ethan, she felt a bit hypersensitive, as if a boogeyman might jump out at her any moment.

I met a real boogeyman once. He's dead.

"I was...out of town," she added, voice a bit breathless as she hurried.

There was a tense pause. "Is everything all right?" Dr. Nelson asked, obviously, he was worrying again.

All right? No, not even close. "Yes," she lied. "It's great." It was way easier to lie to her shrink over the phone than in person.

"Are you planning to come in for a make-up appointment?"

"Actually...no. No, I think I need to take a break." Dr. Nelson had been helpful enough when she'd first started seeing him, but lately... "Thank you for all you've done, but I—"

"Carly, I can tell when you're hiding something from me. I want to help you."

She paused at the crosswalk.

"Come in today. After you get off work. We'll tie up loose ends, and if you want to discontinue your therapy, that is certainly fine with me." There was the faintest hum of sound then he said, "You should know, though, some...visitors have been here, inquiring about you."

The light changed. She didn't move. "What kind of visitors?"

"The FBI."

No, *no.* "You didn't...you didn't tell them anything, did you?"

"Absolutely not," he assured her at once. "You're my patient, but the questions they asked— I'm concerned, Carly. We really must talk."

Jeez. Right. "I'll be there after work." But that would be her last visit. She was sick of poking into that particular wound and sick of being told that she'd always have to face the monster in her mind.

Why couldn't she just shove him into some deep, dark hole and move on?

She pushed the phone into her purse and moments later, she was hurrying down the stairs that would take her to the subway. Her eyes adjusted quickly in the stairwell, and she rushed forward, moving as fast as she could until—

Someone grabbed her. Hard hands yanked her back into the shadows at the base of the stairs. Carly opened her mouth to scream, but a sweaty palm was slapped over her mouth even as the sharp point of a knife pressed into her side. "Not a word," her attacker rasped. "Not a—"

She slammed her high heel down on his tennis shoe. As hard as she could. In the same instant, her elbow plowed back into his stomach. Her attacker's hold eased on her, and Carly screamed—as loudly as she could even as she leapt forward.

"Bitch!" The knife slashed down. Carly saw the glint of the blade coming for her. She didn't stop, but hurtled forward—right into...Ethan?

His hands closed around her and a fast glance at his face showed a mask of cold, absolutely lethal fury. Her heart was pounding frantically in her chest and yes, maybe, she was glad to see him.

"Ethan—" Carly began.

But he had already pushed her behind him and lunged toward her attacker.

That was when Carly realized a crowd had gathered down there. Some people reached out to her, asking if she was okay. Others—well, they stood there, filming the scene with their phones. *What in the hell?*

The man who'd grabbed her tried to run, holding the now cut strap of her purse.

Is that what he was doing when the knife pressed to my side?

Her attacker didn't get far. Ethan caught him by the nape of the neck and yanked the fellow back. "You're not going any damn place."

The attacker whirled around, jabbing out with his knife.

Ethan dodged the attack easily, then caught the guy's wrist. He squeezed that wrist until the attacker screamed. *Did Ethan break the fellow's wrist?*

Someone was calling for the cops. Carly could hear the frantic call, but she couldn't take her eyes off Ethan.

The man who'd attacked her—it wasn't really a man. More of a boy. Long hair. Thin face. Too big clothes. His green eyes were wide with terror as he tried to fight Ethan. It wasn't a battle that the guy would win.

Because with two hits, Ethan had him on the floor. Before he could go for a third punch, Carly called out, "Stop." Her voice had been low, nothing like the excited buzz around her.

But Ethan heard her voice. His fist stilled. His head lifted. His gaze met hers.

"I'm okay," she said.

He bent, grabbed her purse, and strode back toward her.

Just a mugger. Not some crazy ghost from my past. A mugger.

Ethan stood in front of her now. The faint lines near his eyes had deepened, and there was no missing the rage burning in his stare as he held her purse out to her.

Carly took the bag. The knife had sliced right through the strap. She hadn't even felt it when the purse fell away from her shoulder. She'd been too intent on getting away from her attacker. "Thank you."

A muscle jerked in Ethan's jaw.

She glanced around at the crowd. A few people were still filming with their phones, and a uniformed cop was trying to push through the crowd.

Her gaze slid back to Ethan. "You were following me." That was the only explanation for his sudden appearance. And she should be mad—following someone like that definitely qualified as *not normal.* But...

He'd just saved her ass. So it was rather hard to be mad at that particular moment.

His hand lifted, and his fingers brushed over her cheek. She didn't flinch at his touch. In fact, Carly actually felt herself lean into his hand.

Then he pulled away. He turned and just left—without a word.

"Miss!"

Ethan had headed for the stairs.

"Miss!" The cop was beside her now. Ethan was gone. "Miss, I need to find out what happened here..."

What happened? She'd been attacked. Ethan had been there, pulling bodyguard duty and now...

He was gone.

Why do I feel so cold? Why do I want to call him back to me?

Maybe that appointment with her shrink was a better idea than she'd realized. Because wanting to fall back into Ethan's web was a very deadly mistake.

***

Because of the mugging and the resulting too long talk with the cop, Carly was late for work. And as soon as she went inside, she knew that trouble was waiting for her. Because Fiona Rice, her supervisor at the small PR firm, stood just in front of Carly's office door.

Oh, crap.

"Fiona," Carly began quickly. "I can explain..."

She liked Fiona. The woman was intense, a bit edgy, and definitely on the OCD side but—

Fiona waved away her explanation. "You're wanted..." Her voice lowered. "*Upstairs.*"

What?

"You've been requested for the new PR campaign for the Reflections club that is opening in town." Fiona gave a firm nod. "This is huge. So huge. And since I've been training you...the job you do will reflect on me."

So don't screw up!

The other woman didn't say those words, but Carly understood. Completely.

Then Fiona shocked her—the woman grabbed her hand and practically pulled Carly toward the VP elevator. Or at least, that was how Carly thought of it—only the Very Important People at the company ever went up in it.

"There's talk," Fiona told her, voice still hushed, "that the big boss is in town. I've only seen him a few times since he took over the company, so if he's here and you get to meet him..." She blew out a breath. "Tell him how awesome I've been."

"Uh, okay." Fiona had let her go. Carly was in the elevator and she nervously smoothed her hair. She should have gone for the ponytail or a twist that day, something to make her look more sophisticated but she'd been pretty much running on nerves when she dressed and her goal had been to get out of her home as quickly as possible.

Fiona jabbed a button on the elevator and hopped out. "Remember, don't screw this up!" Then she gave Carly a big thumb's up sign.

No screw ups. Check.

The doors closed.

Carly's reflection stared back at her from the mirrored surface of the elevator walls. "I'll try not to screw up," she muttered. But she was pretty much already a serious mess. Her clothes were scuffed and dirty from the attack in the subway. Her hair was definitely disheveled, and her cheeks were way too pale. Hardly the professional image that she wanted to present to the big boss guy. The guy who'd reportedly swooped in and majorly saved the whole place with a buyout. He'd let the employees keep their jobs and he'd pumped a boatload of new cash into the place. Mysterious and rich—that's all she knew about the guy.

The elevator reached the top floor far too quickly, and the doors opened instantly for her. She expected to see one of the assistants waiting for her as she crept out of the elevator.

Instead, Ethan was there.

His hands were shoved in his pockets and when he saw her, his eyebrows lifted—mockingly? "Surprise," he murmured.

She shook her head. And, once more, she looked for an assistant.

But only Ethan was there.

She got a sinking feeling in her stomach. No, absolutely *not*.

The doors began to close. She was more than ready to ride right back downstairs.

Ethan reached out, his hand sliding through the doors and activating the sensors. The doors retreated immediately, and he caught her hand in his. "I think we have an appointment," he said.

Not happening. It's not.

But he was guiding her through the office space and other people she recognized— executives, the power players—were nodding at Ethan as he passed them. They weren't frowning in confusion or wondering why the hell someone as dangerous as Ethan was just strolling around their building.

Because he belongs here. Oh, shit. He belongs.

He took her into one seriously plush office and shut the door behind her. Then she heard the click of the lock. Carly couldn't move. Not so much as an inch. Just breathing was hard.

If he's my boss...if he owns the PR firm...

He owns my brownstone. My apartment.

"You don't own me." Her words were out before she even gave them a second thought.

"No." He sighed. "I don't. But we both know I'd move heaven and earth to possess you."

She whirled for the door, but Ethan was in her path. He didn't touch her, but instead, he lifted his hands, and held them, palms out, in front of her. "Give me a chance to explain."

She wanted to scream. To attack. So she backed away. One step. Another. "You own this firm."

Watching her carefully, Ethan gave a quick nod. "It's a rather...recent acquisition."

She knew that part. The new boss had taken over six months before. *Right after I joined the firm.*

Ethan cleared his throat. "I've been branching out more in the last year. Despite what you may think, none of my business ventures actually have any criminal ties. They're all legit, just like this firm."

Was she supposed to believe him?

He sighed. "Look, fine. So I bought this firm shortly after you were hired. It was struggling, a plum ready for the picking, so I...took it."

The drumming of her heartbeat filled her ears. "You bought it because I was here."

His lips twisted in a half-smile. "Have that much of an opinion of yourself, do you? You really think I'd buy a whole business, just for you?"

She stared at him. "I don't like your games."

His smile faded. "This isn't a game."

Carly rubbed her arms, hating the chill she felt in his office. "Who the hell are you? Ethan Barclay, crime boss? Ethan Barclay, freaking business entrepreneur, Ethan—"

"I'm the man who wants to keep you safe."

"There isn't a threat! The guy at the subway this morning—he was just a desperate kid!"

His gaze flashed. "A kid who could have hurt you."

Now she had to call him on the past. "Don't you remember what it was like to have nothing? To be so desperate that you'd do nearly anything?

Because I do." She'd been desperate enough to take any risk before.

And she'd paid the price for those risks. Her chill was getting worse. "Just how long have you been controlling my life?"

"I'm not—"

"When you called me a few weeks ago and told me that my sister was in danger, I wondered how you'd gotten my number so easily. But I mean, since I was your employee, that was probably easy enough for you to swing, right? You've had total control over me, and I didn't even know it."

A furrow appeared between his brows. "I owe you," he said, his voice deep and intense, "more than I can ever repay. Is it so wrong that when I got a little money, I wanted to help you? This company was going under. I bought it, pumped some capital in...and I saved your job and the job of every person here."

"Ethan..."

"With my background," his laughter was gruff, "trust me, I could use a PR firm of my own. Over the years, I've learned plenty about the value of spin."

Her temples were throbbing. "I don't understand any of this...I just—"

"You didn't pack a bag."

She blinked at the abrupt change in topic. "No."

"And you got up this morning and came to work, as if nothing at all had happened."

"*You're* what has happened to me."

He sucked in a deep breath. "I know."

Wait—what?

Again, that half-smile curved his lips. "But I guess everyone has to have a weakness, right? Even the villains?" Then his knuckles brushed over her cheek. "You're mine. I let others know that, and now we're both in trouble."

"Ethan..."

"I did a lot of thinking after I left you last night. You want to stay here. You want this city. This life. Fine." His hand lingered against her cheek. "But until I'm sure you're safe, you're going to have it *with* me. That's why I made the big reveal at this office today. Why I had to show myself here. Until the danger is past, I'll be here with you. We'll be working together."

Her stomach did a somersault.

"And when it's safe..." His smile slipped. "I can walk away again, if that's what you really want."

What she— "Sometimes, I think you're crazy."

"Of course, I am." His immediate response. "Crazy and very bad for you."

She inched closer to him. "Then why do I feel this way?" She hated it. Loved it. Most of the time, Carly was sure she was walking around in some kind of weird half-life state. Other men didn't make her react this way. Other men just left her cold. But Ethan...

Always, Ethan.

"I want to do right by you," Ethan said, voice soft. "You want to stay here..." His jaw hardened. "Then I am going to stay at your side. I'll make sure any threat that comes your way is eliminated."

"And the FBI?"

"I'll handle them. They've been dodging my steps for years. At this point, I know just how they work." His hand started to drop. Her fingers rose and caught his, holding his hand in place. After not wanting to touch anyone else for so long, she almost felt desperate for *his* touch.

Wrong. Carly knew that the way she felt for him was wrong on a dozen levels.

So what?

"You just have to trust me," Ethan told her. "I'll get you through the storm that's coming."

There was no reason to trust him. He'd deceived her already. She wouldn't be a fool. Wouldn't blindly give in to him.

But...

Her choices were limited. He owned the business, her home, and in this murky world of danger that she found herself in, Carly knew that Ethan understood the risks far more than she did.

So maybe she wouldn't trust him. Maybe she'd use him to get through the darkness heading toward her.

And then she'd figure out just what the hell she needed to do with her life.

Run far and fast from Ethan?

Or stay close.

Carly cleared her throat and tried to get back to some actual business. If it *was* business. "Is the Reflections' campaign even a real thing?"

"Very real." His head bent toward her. "It's a new club I want to open in New York, and you're the PR agent in charge. That is...if you still want to work here. If you don't want to throw the job in my face and walk away."

"I want to walk," she told him. *Did she? Really?* Carly wasn't even certain. "But I can't. So tell me about this job..." She let his hand go. She tried to focus on business and not on the way he made her feel.

Ethan...he knew all her secret shames. All of her pains and her needs.

And Ethan...he was the one man she shouldn't let get close to her.

So why was he the one she wanted most?

***

It had worked. At six o'clock that evening, Ethan watched the city below him. Most people were heading out—it was the weekend, after all. Time for them to get loose and wild. Or maybe just time to relax.

Carly hadn't left yet. She'd stayed at the office all day, working hard on plans for Reflections. Before his big reveal to her, he'd wondered if she'd run the instant she saw him. He'd been prepared to chase her. But she hadn't run.

She hadn't slapped him, either. Another win.

She'd just stood there, so heart-breakingly beautiful, and she'd nearly gutted him, just with a look.

Hurt. Betrayal. Everything he did was to protect her, but Carly didn't see that. She just saw pain. She saw him.

Maybe that was all he was to her. Pain.

Maybe he should have stayed a memory for her, nothing more but—

A knock sounded at his door. "Come in," he called, without glancing back. He figured it was his assistant, coming in with a last check of the day.

But when the door creaked open, the faintest sweet scent drifted to him. Her scent. His eyes closed for a second, and his hands fisted in front of him.

Don't hurt her again. Whatever the hell you do, don't hurt her.

"So..." Her voice reached him easily. "What's supposed to happen now? Are you going to be my shadow all weekend? From this threat that I don't actually see coming?"

He turned to face her.

"I don't know how you intend for this to work." She stood in his doorway, looking uncertain and far too lovely.

Don't fuck up. Don't.

"Just who is it that you think will be coming after me?"

"Quincy Atkins had a brother. One who didn't exactly take it well when the guy vanished." He saw her shoulders tense. "Unfortunately, I learned that Daniel Duvato was trying to contact that guy...shortly before Daniel's rather well-deserved death."

"You think the brother will come after me?"

"I think I want you safe, and I don't want to take chances."

She seemed to absorb that.

"As for this weekend...I thought you might want to come with me and see Reflections. I mean, it is your project. So getting a first-hand look at the place should benefit you." He tried to sound casual. Not like he was offering her a date. That would be sleazy, all things considered.

Right? Or would she be open to—

She looked down at her watch. "I-I have an...appointment first. But then I'd love to see the place."

What kind of appointment? He bit back the question.

Her gaze slid toward him. "Don't worry. I'm not meeting with the FBI."

"Never said you were," he murmured.

"Don't lie," she chided him. "Special Agent Monroe called me twice today, and I refused to talk to him both times." She sighed softly. "The guy is going to keep dodging my steps."

He'd have to deal with Monroe.

"I'm not ready to talk with him." She firmed her shoulders. "But I do have another meeting that can't be delayed."

A meeting? Or a date?

"I'll have my driver take you over." After her attack this morning, the last thing he wanted was for her to be out alone.

"Thank you," Carly said. "I'd...appreciate that."

Shock rolled through him.

"What?" Carly asked, tilting her head to the side so her hair slid over her shoulder. "Did you think I wouldn't appreciate a ride? Seriously,

Ethan, my day has sucked. Getting a ride in a fancy car isn't something I'm going to argue about."

Great. Then maybe she wouldn't argue when she realized he was going with her.

He grabbed his briefcase and headed for the door. He wanted to take her hand, but he controlled that impulse. For her, he would try and act the gentleman.

She'd been willing to kill in order to keep him safe. A man never forgot a woman who'd done that for him.

They rode down the elevator in silence, and when they headed through the glass doors of the building and out into the busy city streets, he wasn't particularly surprised to see Agent Monroe standing at the corner.

But when Monroe saw him, the guy glowered.

Ethan's car was waiting right out front. As Ethan opened the door for Carly, he gave the special agent a friendly wave...

With his middle finger. Then he climbed in the car after her. The door shut with a soft thud and Carly gave him their destination address.

When they pulled away from the curb, he didn't look back to see if the FBI agent was following him or not. Right then, he wasn't doing anything that would get him in trouble.

That part would come later.

***

Having a car take her through the city was nearly heaven to Carly. Traffic was insane, of course, but then, it was New York, so how could it be anything else? But when Ethan's driver pulled to a stop in front of Dr. Nelson's building, he didn't seem to have any trouble finding a place to park. Mostly because Carly realized the guy had just *made* a spot for the sleek car.

A privacy screen separated them from the driver, and that screen had made her feel far too conscious of her close proximity to Ethan.

"Who are you meeting?" Ethan asked her.

Her hand had already gone to the door handle, but she hesitated. "You know so much about my life. Surely you know this part, too?" And she hated that. Hated that her soul was so bare. "If this is going to work..." Carly didn't even know that *this* was, not yet. An uneasy relationship? An alliance? She cleared her throat. "If we're going to get through the next few days, I really think it would be better if we didn't lie to each other."

His fingers feathered over her shoulder. "I'm not lying to you. I have no fucking clue who is waiting in that building. It could be a lover. It could be a PI. I own the public relations company, yes, but I didn't push into your whole life."

Didn't you? It sure felt that way to her. She was so unbalanced, so unsettled...and maybe that was why the truth came out. "Quincy broke a part of me." That was the way she'd felt. "Before you got there that night...before you broke in..." *Say it. Say it.* "He raped me."

The silence in that car was stark. Stunning. Terrifying.

She opened the door and risked a glance back at Ethan. The car's interior light shone down on him, and he'd gone absolutely white. The only color in his face was his blazing eyes.

"I know you suspected." He'd arrived after she'd already been attacked. But this—this was the first time she'd ever said those stark words to him.

His hands were clenched at his sides.

"You and I, we didn't talk again, after that night..." Her heart was slamming into her chest. *Get out of the car.* But she didn't move. "It was hard to get over it." *Why am I lying? It wasn't hard. Freaking impossible. I still hurt.*

"Baby," his voice was a rasp. "You're ripping out my heart. I've wished a fucking thousand times I'd gotten there sooner."

She shook her head. "Then maybe his men just would've killed you." Quincy almost *had* killed him. "I don't blame you. I-I hope you know that."

"I blame my fucking self."

She had to blink away the tears that wanted to fill her eyes.

"If I could," Ethan continued, his voice still so rough and ragged. "I would kill that bastard again. Only it would be slower. And he'd beg for the end."

She shook her head. Hard. "That isn't the way. It isn't the way to get better." And she *was* better. A nightmare hadn't woken her up in weeks. So she still had trouble getting close to men. At least she didn't vomit after a man touched her. She'd done that, the first time she'd gone out on a date after the attack.

But then she'd started her therapy. She'd been determined not to let Quincy or his ghost win.

And he won't.

Maybe something had broken inside of her, but she'd rebuilt herself. Piece by piece. "My shrink is in that office. Dr. Nelson. I've had therapy, on and off, since the attack." Dr. Nelson was the therapist she'd started to see after her last doctor had moved out of town. She'd been seeing Dr. Nelson for about seven months, but...

But this is the end now.

She put her heel down on the pavement. One, then the other, and she slid out of the car. The driver stood a few feet away, waiting, no expression on his face. "You okay?"

"Yes, fine. Thank you. For asking...and, um, for the ride." Carly nodded to him. "I'm Carly, by the way." She'd been so nervous before that she hadn't introduced herself to him. Ethan had a way of doing that—making her forget pretty much everything else.

"Charles." His head inclined toward her and he gave her a brief smile.

She wanted to smile back, but her emotions were spinning out of control. She'd lied when she told Charles that she was fine. *Fine* wasn't even an option.

Carly could hear Ethan behind her. Climbing from the car. Part of her wanted to break and run away. Another part wanted to see just what he'd say to her.

She'd never told another lover the truth before.

He isn't your lover. You shared some hot kisses with him long ago. And, okay, maybe recently, too. But he isn't—

He turned her toward him. His hands were gentle on her. So incredibly gentle. Ethan's fingers curled under her chin as he tipped her head back and she stared into his eyes.

"I should have gotten there sooner."

Carly shook her head. No, hadn't Ethan heard her? The attack hadn't been on him. Quincy had been a sick, twisted psychopath. He'd—

"No one will hurt you again, Carly. If they try..." He bent and kissed her. Softly. Carefully. Like she was some delicate treasure to him.

She wasn't, of course. But...

"If anyone tries," he whispered against her lips, "I will fucking make him wish for death."

Such a gentle touch, such a terrifying promise...because she knew he meant those words.

"You are perfect. Know that. Always have been. Always will be," Ethan said as his forehead pressed to hers. He just—held her there, with traffic around them, with people hurrying past on the sidewalk.

"You sent me away," Carly whispered. He probably didn't know about her trip to the psych ward. Now wasn't the time for that bombshell. One painful past reveal was enough sharing for the moment.

He flinched. "I thought I was helping you...Getting you away from me and the danger in D.C."

But she'd needed him. So much.

Why had she called out for him in that psych ward? What had she really thought that Ethan would do for her?

"I hope you understand," he whispered into her ear. "I hope you know...you *are* still perfect. Still strong and good, and that bastard didn't do anything to alter who *you* are."

Her arms were around him. She was holding him just as tightly. The tears were back, and she didn't stop them. So what if a crowd could see them? She needed this moment. She needed Ethan. A man who knew all of her secrets and still told her—

You are still perfect.

"I missed you," she confessed to him. Probably a huge mistake, but she was past the point of being able to stop. Their relationship— good, bad, fucked up—it went too deep for her to hide that truth from him.

"And I think part of me might have just died without you," he told her.

Her breath caught in her throat. She looked up at him.

"You were always the best thing in my life," Ethan said. "*You* were the good one. And without you...you don't really want to know what I became."

She wanted to know everything about him.

"Go on inside," Ethan told her. "I'll be waiting for you when you come out."

Right. Her appointment. Dr. Nelson.

Slowly, she pulled away from Ethan. Her gaze searched his once more, and she was surprised because she could have sworn that she saw a flash of pain in his eyes.

Ethan...in pain.

That was something she'd never liked. "I'm okay now," she told him, oddly driven to comfort him.

He gave her a slow smile. "Baby, you always have been. Even at seventeen, you were the strongest woman I'd ever seen."

Her heart raced faster as she turned away from him. There were tears on her cheeks, but for some reason, her steps seemed lighter as she hurried to her appointment with Dr. Nelson.

***

Ethan watched Carly until she'd disappeared into the tall, gleaming building. He pulled in a deep breath, one that seemed to hurt his lungs. His hands had fisted when she walked away, and he wanted, so badly, to drive those fists hard and deep into—

"Uh, Ethan?"

He turned at the question and found his new driver/bodyguard watching him with worried eyes.

Charles West was dressed in a light blazer and jeans. His dark eyes showed a hint of worry as he glanced from Ethan toward the building. "Is everything all right, boss?"

He was sure Charles had overheard plenty. The tall, deceptively strong, African American guy had many talents—and few weaknesses. Ethan respected the fellow for a whole hell of a lot of reasons, but he didn't trust him. Not even close.

"I really want to fucking kill someone," Ethan said.

Charles tensed. A brief movement, but a telling one.

"Got a particular target in mind?" Charles asked carefully.

That was probably what the guy was supposed to say. No judgment. He didn't get paid for judgment. He got paid to make sure that Ethan stayed alive. Not to be his conscience.

"Yeah," Ethan said. "I do." *Pity a man can only die once.* But though most of his rage was directed at Quincy, a whole lot of that fury was turned straight at...*me.*

Carly had been alone after that attack. Alone because Ethan had stupidly believed sending her away would keep her safe. He'd wanted her out of the city so that no suspicion would ever be put on her.

He'd also thought—hell, that she wouldn't want to see him right then. Not knowing...*I drove that knife into the bastard's heart with no hesitation.*

Now the suspicion was on her and the pain—she'd carried it alone for years.

"Boss, is someone dying tonight?"

He tilted back his head. "Someone dies every night."

Wasn't that the sad fucking truth?

CHAPTER THREE

"You shouldn't have missed your appointment," Dr. Keith Nelson's voice held a chiding edge that Carly really didn't like.

Considering that she'd missed the appointment because she'd been in the hospital, she certainly didn't need his little guilt trip.

"It's important for your progress," he continued, his handsome face showing a delicate concern, "for you to keep meeting with me. You know you need—"

"This is my last session." There. Bombshell dropped.

Behind the frames of his glasses, his green eyes widened. "That's not something I can condone."

There was *something* about Dr. Keith that had been bothering her for a while. She could never really relax in his presence. It was odd, but...he made her feel on edge.

Though she didn't exactly know why.

Dr. Keith Nelson had come with the highest possible recommendation from her previous psychiatrist. He was an up-and-coming therapist with a thriving practice. Dr. Nelson was in his mid-thirties, with thick, blond hair, and a handsome but serious face. The glasses he wore—they gave him a distinguished air, though she'd secretly started to suspect he wore those glasses *just* for that air.

"Does this have anything to do..." Dr. Nelson asked her, "with the gentleman I saw you embracing outside of the building?"

She tried not to let her surprise show. The shrink had been watching that scene?

"Because," he continued before she could respond, "I saw that you let him touch you, and touch has been such a very big issue for you to overcome."

The ticking of the clock on the wall seemed incredibly loud. "This isn't about Ethan."

"Ethan." He paused, then said, "Your voice softens when you say his name. You already feel a-a connection with him?"

The problem with shrinks—they could see too much. And when she felt like hiding, that wasn't a good thing.

"Do you really believe you're ready for a normal relationship?" Dr. Nelson pressed.

At that question, she had to laugh. "Who said anything about normal?" Normal wasn't for her. She'd realized that long ago. Carly rose from the couch and paced to the window. When she looked down, yes, she could see Ethan's car. But there was no sign of Ethan. Was he waiting inside the vehicle for her, shielded behind those tinted windows? Her hand lifted and touched the glass.

"Normal is overrated. It's not what I need. I've realized that." She'd tried to stick herself in a normal world for so long, and she'd felt nothing. But when Ethan had come back into her life...

"Does he know about your attack?"

"Yes."

Silence. Then... "While I applaud the level of intimacy you're reaching by sharing with your new partner, I must caution you to—"

"No more caution. I've had plenty of caution." Brisk now, she turned away from the window and faced the psychiatrist. When had he moved so close to her? "Thanks for all of your help, but I'm going to be taking a—"

He caught her hands in his. She flinched instantly and tried to draw back, but he held her tightly. "Do you see this?"

"Take your hands off me." Her voice was flat.

"You aren't done with therapy. You still tense up when I get too close—when most men do."

Not Ethan.

His eyes narrowed behind the lenses of his glasses, as if he'd just read her thoughts. *Isn't that what shrinks are supposed to do? Know the patients, inside and out?* "So you found one man who doesn't scare you," he said. "What happens when you're done with him? Or when he's done with you? I can help you. You need *me*."

"Right now, I need you to let go of my hands." She wasn't going to say it again. If she had to do it, she'd be kneeing him in the groin or shoving her high heel down on his foot, just like she'd done to her attacker in the subway.

His lips parted. He glanced down at her hands. His fingers slid up, almost...caressing her wrists.

That one touch—it was wrong. She knew it with utter certainty. A caress. Far too intimate for a doctor to give his patient. *It felt wrong.*

She jerked away from him. "Trust me, I don't need you." She should have listened to her instincts with him long ago.

Shock had slackened his face. "Carly, I didn't mean—" He broke off as heat stained his cheeks. "I'm sorry. I-I overstepped."

And it was time for her to step out. "Bill me," Carly said as she marched briskly for the door. "Because we are done." Then she yanked open the door and swept past the empty reception area. As soon as she entered the elevator, she whirled back around because she'd heard the rush of footsteps following her.

"Carly, please!" Now Dr. Nelson's voice broke a bit. "Let me explain."

Blindly, she jabbed the buttons on the elevator. She wanted those damn doors to close.

"I...I feel deeply for you, Carly. I didn't plan it, I—"

The doors closed before she could hear any more of his confession.

She sagged back. Some days were bad. Some days...were freaking insane.

***

Ethan's fingers drummed against his knee. Carly hadn't been inside the building very long. Maybe ten minutes, fifteen max.

So why was an edge of worry knifing through him?

He opened his door and glanced up at the building. Charles was still seated in the front of the vehicle. They weren't exactly parked legally there, and when he glanced to the right, Ethan saw a cop approaching. Figured. Cops could usually smell him from a mile away.

"Drive around the block," Ethan ordered Charles. "We'll be waiting when you come back."

Then he straightened and headed to the building. Maybe he was curious about the shrink—or maybe, hell, he was just curious about Carly.

And I want to be close to her. She was hurting when she left me.

He wanted to take away all of her pain. No, he *needed* to take it away. He entered the lobby and scanned the list of posted businesses on the building's directory.

Ah...there he was. Dr. Nelson. Dr. Keith Nelson. Seventh floor.

The building already seemed pretty deserted, so Ethan didn't have to wait long for an elevator to arrive. He gave a little nod to the security guy who glanced his way, then Ethan slipped into the elevator. Time to meet Dr. Nelson.

***

The elevator doors opened. Carly immediately shot outside, but then three steps later, she stopped as she finally took note of her surroundings.

She wasn't in the lobby.

She was in the parking garage.

A car horn's echo reached her ears. Most of the spaces in the garage were empty, and the place seemed strangely dark.

She turned back toward the elevator. The doors were already starting to close and she jabbed for the button to open them once more. The button lit up beneath her touch and the doors began to open fully.

"Carly."

Her shoulders tensed. Had she just heard her name? Or had she imagined that? She risked a quick glance over her shoulder.

And that was when she saw the man. Tall. Wide shoulders. Wearing a black ski mask. He'd just appeared from behind the nearby cement column.

She didn't waste time on a scream. Instead, Carly shot toward the open doors of that elevator. She made it inside and turned for the control panel.

But he rushed in right behind her. He grabbed her, holding her tightly with his gloved hands. "Knew I just had to wait...long enough..." His voice was a low growl. "And you'd be mine."

She twisted and kicked, punching out at him, but he held her tightly and he—he hauled her out of the elevator.

Carly screamed, as loudly as she could.

Too bad no one was around to hear her scream.

Again. It's happening again. Because a man in a mask had come for her once before...one of Quincy's goons who'd abducted her.

And back then, there'd been no one to hear her screams, either.

***

When the elevator stopped on the seventh floor, Ethan entered the hallway and walked slowly toward Dr. Nelson's office. Gold lettering gleamed on the guy's door. Ethan didn't bother to knock. Instead, he opened the door and stepped into the reception area. No one was there.

The shrink needed better security. Much, much better. Just anyone could walk right inside.

Anyone had.

Another door waited just a few steps away. The shrink's inner sanctum. Was Carly inside with him?

But then that other door opened. A man stood there, the light glinting off his glasses. He was a few inches shorter than Ethan, his body thinner.

"You!" The guy said, his eyes widening as he took a step back. "What are you—did Carly tell you what happened? Dammit, she sent you up here fast!"

Okay, the doctor knew him. How—they'd get to that part later. Right now...

He really didn't like the guy's tone. Ethan stalked forward.

"No!" The doctor threw his hands up. "It was a mistake, I swear! I didn't mean—I wasn't hitting on her."

Fucking asshole. Ethan had already been in the mood for some violence before, and now this jerkoff was about to push him too far. "You're her shrink," Ethan gritted out.

"Not anymore." The guy's Adam's apple bobbed. "Carly discontinued therapy. And that's not a good idea."

"It is if her asshole shrink is hitting on her."

The asshole in question flinched. "I know her, okay? And I saw the two of you together down there—I just wanted to warn her what a mistake she was making. She didn't have to run to you and tell you what happened!"

Run to you. Actually, he rather wished Carly would run to him. All the damn time.

She's not here with the doc. She left, no doubt upset. But he hadn't seen her in the lobby. Had she been on a different elevator?

Without another word, Ethan turned away from the shrink. It was better to get away from him, far less tempting that way. If he lingered, he just might drive his fist into the man's nose. *Hitting on Carly—her shrink!* She'd probably trusted the guy. Fuck.

He marched back into the hallway and headed for the elevator.

The fool was following him, nearly begging to get his face smashed in.

"She misunderstood the situation!" The doctor was huffing and puffing behind him. "That's all! I would never take advantage of a patient."

Ethan spun to face him. "You sure as hell had better not."

The doctor's mouth hung open.

Ethan gave him a cold smile. "You have no clue who I am, do you?" He realized this now. "You just saw me kissing Carly, and you figure I'm the boyfriend..."

"Aren't you?" The shrink squared his shoulders. "You don't know about *her*, okay? You don't know...what she's capable of doing."

"Actually, I do."

"No—you know the surface, that's it! I've been trying to break through with her, but she deflects—"

"You're a real damn chatty bastard, aren't you? Doesn't client confidentiality matter at all to you? Or are you just trying to drive me away from Carly because you stupidly think you have a shot with her?"

"I-I—"

"You don't know me," Ethan told him. "And you should really hope that you *never* see me again. Because if you do...then that means I'm there for one reason." He gave the shrink a cold smile. "To kick your ass."

"I-I—" His face flushed. "I'll call the cops."

Ethan gave a low laugh. "Right. 'Cause they'll keep you safe from me." He gave a little salute. "You have your warning."

He went into the elevator. The other man watched him with wide eyes. "You're so wrong for her," the shrink said. "She can't—she shouldn't be with someone like you."

The doors were about to close. "Hey, doc," Ethan called.

The man's chin jerked.

"Fuck off," Ethan said. The doors slid closed.

Bastard. Carly had gone to him for help, and what—the SOB had just been lusting after her? Maybe he should go back and teach the guy some well-deserved manners. A guy with that many degrees should have enough sense to treat a woman right—and not hit on a vulnerable patient.

I will kick his ass. The elevator doors opened. But a quick sweep of the lobby showed that only the guard was there.

Ethan forgot the dick shrink—for the moment—and strode toward the guard. "Gorgeous red-head, about five foot five, blue eyes." His words came out rapid-fire.

The guard nodded. "I saw her come up."

"When did she leave?"

The guard hesitated. "Just who are—"

"*When did she leave?*"

The guard swallowed. His hand nervously slid toward the radio on his hip. "I haven't seen that lady leave."

But—she should have left by then. He'd had time to go upstairs and come back down. Something was wrong with this scene. Very, very wrong.

"I'll like to see your ID, sir," the guard told him as he gave a grim nod.

"Is there a parking garage in this building?" Because if someone had taken Carly, then that person would have needed a different way to get her out.

Unless she isn't being taken. Maybe she's just being...killed.

"Yeah, yeah, there's a garage below—"

Ethan didn't stand around to hear anymore. He ran right for the stairwell that waited on the left. The stairwell was closer than the elevator.

The guard shouted, "I need your ID!"

"Screw that—just call the cops! A woman is missing!" Maybe he was jumping the gun, but he didn't care. Not with the danger that was his life— the danger that he knew was stalking Carly. He'd thought she would be safe in the shrink's office. That mistake was on him. Now he had to find her, fast.

Ethan threw open that stairwell door and raced down the steps.

***

He had the knife at her neck, but he wasn't slicing open her throat.

"Make another sound," the attacker said, his voice chilling her, "and I swear, you will never talk again."

Her screams had stopped.

They were beside the back of a van. Big, black. The kind of van that had always made her instantly think...*serial killer*.

"We're going for a little ride. And when that ride stops..."

What? She'd be dead? Because Carly knew—with absolute certainty—that if she got in the van, she was a dead woman. She'd read some study about that somewhere. Online. In some magazine. *Somewhere*. You were never supposed to get in the car and be taken from the scene—that decreased your survival chances too much.

She'd been taken before. When she'd been seventeen. She'd wound up with Quincy, hurting. Trapped.

It couldn't happen again.

I just need someone else to come out of the elevator. I need someone to see me. Even Dr. Nelson would be a welcome sight right then.

"When the ride stops, you'll pay for what you did."

Definitely going to kill me. So she had to move, and she had to move fast.

Because the elevator wasn't opening. No one was rushing to her rescue. If she wanted to live, then she had to save herself.

"That's right, don't fight," he said, sounding pleased. With one hand, he yanked open the back door of the van. She saw a rope inside. Handcuffs. Duct tape. Everything a good serial killer would need. "Knew you'd be a good girl..."

She punched her fist into his side, as hard as she could. She'd never been the good girl. She'd been the one breaking the rules, sneaking out, taking risks.

And even if she hadn't...*Good girls know how to fight back, too.*

He yelled when she hit him. Carly lunged forward even as she felt the blade slice across her—not her neck, but closer to her collarbone and then—

"Carly!" That fierce roar seemed to shake the entire parking garage. She knew that roar. Ethan. He'd found her.

"Ethan!" She yelled back for him as loudly as she could. She wasn't going to be quiet. Wasn't going to be good. She surged forward, even though she fully expected to feel another slash from that knife.

Only...

There wasn't a slash. Her high heels clattered across the cement and she rushed toward Ethan. He was running out of the stairwell, and she had never been so happy to see anyone in her entire life.

Then she heard the squeal of tires. At that sound, she glanced to the right. The van was barreling toward her. The headlights were so bright as they shone onto her, blinding her for a moment. Her attacker wasn't coming after her with a knife. He was trying to run her down with his freaking van.

"Carly!" Ethan grabbed her hand and they went flying together, rolling hard when they hit the cement and tumbling over, again and again.

The van sped past them, never slowing and taking the curve on two wheels as it rushed toward the exit.

The squeal of tires echoed like a scream around her. Her body hurt—probably because she'd slammed into cement *and* Ethan's hard body. Her breath heaved out, and she fought to calm her frantic heartbeat.

"Baby, baby, please, talk to me."

She blinked and saw Ethan's face right above hers. He was staring at her with desperate eyes. A desperate Ethan—a sight she didn't see every day. "Wh-what do you want me to say?" *A crazy man just attacked me. He scared the hell out of me.* That pretty much summed up the last ten minutes of her day.

"You're bleeding." His hand flew toward her collarbone. "Sonofabitch. It's okay. I've got you. It's going to be okay."

"Ethan..."

"I have to see how bad it is."

She almost didn't want to know. Not if it *was* bad, anyway. "He's...getting away." The man she'd never seen—the man in the mask. The man who'd said that he'd been waiting for her. Waiting with duct tape and handcuffs.

Suddenly, the threats that Ethan had mentioned were horribly, terrifyingly real.

Ethan kept one hand on her collarbone even as he yanked out his phone with the other. His fingers flew across the screen. "Charles, I need an ambulance. Yes, I said a fucking ambulance. No, no, shit, I didn't kill anyone. It's Carly." His fingers pressed a bit harder to her skin. "Some bastard attacked her. We're in the parking garage. *He's* getting away. In a black van, late model, driving hell fast. Find the SOB. Stop him." Then he dropped the phone. "I'm going to pick you up," he told Carly. "I'll take you outside. Charles will get the ambulance, and everything will be okay."

"Liar." Things were far from okay.

He lifted her into his arms. Held her carefully and turned—

"What in the hell is happening?"

She didn't recognize that horrified voice, but when her gaze slid to the speaker, she saw a man in a guard's uniform. Wait, was he pointing pepper spray at them?

"An attack just happened," Ethan snarled back. "I told you to get the cops here. She's hurt, and some jerk in a black van is getting away."

The guard's face went slack with shock. But, before he could say anything else, more men were rushing out of the stairwell behind him. Armed men.

Men in...FBI vests?

She saw Special Agent Monroe. He was at the front of that pack. He closed in and as he did, he aimed his gun right at Ethan.

"What the fuck have you done now?" Agent Monroe demanded.

***

The bitch. The bitch. The *bitch*.

He drove into another parking garage, moving as fast as he could, and he ditched that van. Just jumped out of it and ran into the shadows.

He wasn't about to take off his ski mask. Not with the chance that his image might be caught on a security camera. It was a good damn thing he'd worn gloves. At least there wouldn't be any fingerprints in the van—he figured the cops would find it, sooner or later.

He yanked at the handles on a few nearby cars, and alarms started peeling. Shit. He didn't need this—

One car didn't sound an alarm. One car...it was actually unlocked.

He glanced at the plates. *Tourist.*

Some people should really know better.

He jumped in the car, and, less than a minute later, he was shooting out of that parking garage. When it was safe, he ditched the ski mask.

His ribs fucking hurt from her hit. She'd pay for that attack. He was going to make sure of it. She'd be paying for everything that she'd done to him.

Did she think retribution would never come her way? Oh, it would.

Revenge. Punishment. Hell.

Carly Shay would get exactly what was due to her.

CHAPTER FOUR

The wound hadn't been deep enough for stitches. Apparently, she just had a tendency to bleed like crazy. Who knew?

Carly sat on a gurney in the ER, a paper gown covering her body. Her clothes had been taken—where, she didn't really know. Though she suspected the FBI had confiscated them. Probably looking for some kind of evidence on them.

Had the attacker bled on her? It was possible. She'd sure tried to hurt him. So maybe the FBI had his blood, his DNA. Maybe they could find out who the jerk was.

The curtains around her were pushed aside, and Carly gave a quick jump.

"Easy." Ethan's voice was low. "It's just me."

Her heartbeat didn't slow down any.

Her bare feet flexed a bit and her shoulders hunched. "I figured the FBI would be hauling you away."

He laughed and came closer. "They can't. They don't have any evidence to use against me. Story of their lives." His hand lifted and he brushed back her hair. When she glanced at his face, Carly saw that his laughter was already gone, as if it had never been there at all.

His expression was so intent that her breath caught for a moment. *What's wrong now?*

His gaze dropped to her new bandage. "I was scared as all hell when I couldn't find you in that building. I went up to that idiot shrink's office and found out that you were gone, but the guard in the lobby said you hadn't left."

She swallowed, then focused on breathing. Nice and easy. "So you came in, guns blazing, to find me." She could hear the bustle of people around her. Doctors and nurses were working frantically just behind the curtain. She'd been told that she had to stay put, for a few more moments, until her doctor officially released her.

She didn't want to wait, though. Carly wanted to cut and run.

Hospitals weren't exactly her favorite spots.

"I should have been with you the whole time. I knew the threat was there. I knew that Quincy's brother was looking for you."

"You still think it was the brother?"

"I think his younger brother, Curtis, has been aiming to punish his brother's killer for years. He might look clean on paper, but I know better—than just about anyone else—how easy it is to fake a clean cover."

"I didn't see his face. I have no clue who attacked me." She gave a weak laugh. "The FBI agent grilled me, again and again, but I couldn't tell him much. Just that the guy was big, close to your height. Strong. His voice was low, no accent that I could detect." And all that was pretty much nothing. No useful info. "He had all of his killing supplies in the back of that van. He said he'd been waiting to get me alone—"

"He *won't* get you alone again," Ethan promised her.

"You can't stay with me forever."

"Don't be so sure about that."

The curtain slid back once more. This time, her doctor was there. And a male nurse—one holding scrubs and looking apologetic.

"I'm sorry," the nurse began, "but you won't be getting your clothes back tonight. The FBI—"

"Right," Carly interrupted. "I figured that." But at least the nurse had brought her scrubs to wear. She wouldn't be heading out in the paper gown and flashing her ass to the FBI agents on the way out of the hospital.

That was one win for her.

Maybe.

"The wound wasn't severe," the doctor said. The doctor was a lady who appeared to be in her late twenties, maybe early thirties. A little too thin and with her blonde hair pulled back in a ponytail. "Just keep it clean. The last thing you want is an infection."

Actually, the last thing she wanted was to be hunted by some psycho with serial killing supplies at the ready, but yes, an infection was bad, too.

"It may scar," the doctor said. And as she said those words, the doctor's gaze cut to Ethan's face, then, quickly, she looked away. "Though scarring can be minimalized by—"

"I don't care about scars," Carly responded flatly. "I care about breathing. He missed my jugular, so I know just how lucky I am."

The doctor glanced down at her chart. "You're clear to go. If you have any issues, just give us a call back."

Ethan had taken the scrubs from the nurse. A call back? Hopefully not.

The doctor and nurse left. Ethan put the scrubs on the gurney beside her. Voices drifted in and out.

"I need to change," Carly said. "So you have to leave."

He put his hands on either side of her body. "You never look at my scars."

His scars. The slashes that slid down each of his cheeks.

"You've never asked about them, either. Don't you want to know how I got them?" He leaned in closer. "Daniel Duvato gave them to me. The man I'd trusted for years—he hated me. And he had been working to make my life a living hell. Anytime I got close to a woman, he attacked her. He was setting me up, you see. Making it look as if I were some insane killer. And at the end, when he snapped completely, he came after me. Stabbed me again and again." He caught her hand. Pressed it to his chest. "I've got more scars than I care to count. He wanted the world to look at me and see that I was a monster. As twisted on the outside as I was on the inside."

She shook her head. "You aren't."

"Ah, baby, we both know that's a lie."

"You *aren't.*" And the other voices faded away. "You're right—I didn't ask about your scars. Mostly because I don't see them. You're handsome as sin, and you have to know that, Ethan. Women look at you, and I'm pretty sure panties drop. There's nothing twisted about how you look. There's nothing twisted about *you.*"

His face softened. "Oh, Carly, if only that were true." He brought her hand up to his mouth and pressed a kiss to her palm. "I'll turn my back while you dress, but I don't want to leave. Now that I finally pushed my way past the FBI, I don't plan to leave you for a very long time."

Because he thought the attacker might strike again? Fear bloomed in her stomach and she hurriedly dressed. In her head, she kept sliding back into that parking garage. Kept seeing the man in that ski mask coming at her.

Ethan's shoulders seemed so incredibly tense as he stood there, just in front of the thin curtain. She glanced down at her toes, feeling vulnerable in the scrubs. What was she supposed to do about her shoes? They'd given her some little sock things and she put those on quickly, but it wasn't as if those were really going to help her once she left the hospital. "I need to get back to my place," she said. "Will you get Charles to take me there?"

He turned toward her. "No."

Her brows lifted. "I have to go home, Ethan. I can't hide forever."

His jaw hardened. "Why don't you stay with me tonight?"

She was pretty sure her heart nearly shot right out of her chest.

"No sex." A muscle flexed along the hard line of his jaw. "That's not what I'm saying."

Well, damn. The one man she actually wanted and—what, now he was going to treat her with kid gloves? Because of her confession about the rape? Or because she was now sporting a lovely bandage courtesy of her attacker?

"I want to make sure you're safe. I *owe* you—"

Again with the owing. At that one word, *owe*, her temper erupted. Without another word to him, Carly shoved aside the curtain and marched out of the emergency room. She kept her gaze straight ahead, but with her peripheral vision, she could see some of the other patients in the ER. One man was a bloody mess—had he been in a traffic accident? And there was a crying kid to the left. It looked as if he'd broken his leg.

A woman had a long slice along her thigh and—

I'm out of there. She shoved open the emergency room doors and exhaled a hard sigh of relief. Only that relief didn't exactly last long because she made a beeline for the swinging doors of the hospital's exit, and when she stepped foot outside the place, FBI Special Agent Victor Monroe appeared.

Did he seriously have nothing better to do than track her?

"You didn't think you'd just disappear into the night, did you?" he asked her.

She took a step back and hit something—someone. Even before his hands settled around her shoulders, she knew that Ethan was behind her. She knew his smell—that rich, masculine scent. And his touch—she'd be able to recognize his touch anywhere, anytime.

"I'm not disappearing," she said. She'd already talked to the agent, again and again, while the docs had examined her. "I'm just going home."

But the agent's gaze cut up to Ethan's. "Is she now?"

"That's what she wants," Ethan said flatly.

Victor's expression hardened. "My mistake," he murmured. "I thought you cared about this one. Guess my intel was wrong."

Ethan's hold tightened on her. His fingers were close to her wound, but not touching it, thank goodness. She probably would have freaked if he'd hit that spot with a careless touch. Since the agent was now studying her so intently, she made herself give a light laugh. "I have no idea where that faulty intel is coming from, but obviously Ethan doesn't care about me."

Victor glanced at her shoulders. At Ethan's hands. Slowly, his gaze slid back to her face, then to Ethan's. "My mistake." Same words, but his tone had changed now. "I just would have thought that with an imminent threat against you, Ethan would want to make certain you were in a secure location. I highly doubt that your home is a safe place."

Her palms were starting to sweat. "I have an alarm system."

"A professional came after you tonight."

She realized that. The serial killing tools had been a dead giveaway. Not like it had been amateur hour.

"You really think some standard grade alarm will keep him away?" Victor shook his head. "It won't. But I can keep you safe. The FBI will provide you ample protection."

Will you still protect me when you realize I killed Quincy Atkins? She exhaled slowly. The pavement was cutting through the bottom of her loaner socks. And she felt far too exposed just wearing those oversized scrubs. "In return for this protection, you expect me to—what?"

"To tell the truth."

I don't like the truth. I like to pretend my past doesn't exist.

Schooling her expression, Carly said, "I don't have any information that can help you. I don't know who is after me."

"*He* does," Victor said.

And at that, Ethan moved to Carly's side. They were just a few feet from the hospital doors, and the light from the hospital poured down on them.

"You know plenty, don't you, Ethan?" Victor pressed. "You knew she'd be a wanted woman and that's why you hauled ass up here. My mistake was in believing that it was because you cared about her. Now I get it, though. You're here because you want to stop her from talking. Why? Because you're afraid she'll incriminate you? Afraid that you'll finally find yourself on the inside of a jail cell for all the twisted shit you've—"

"*Stop.*" The angry snarl tore from Carly.

Victor's words immediately fell away into silence.

"You don't know Ethan." And it was as if a volcano had burst inside of her. She couldn't contain herself. "You know the stories. The crap his enemies want you to believe. But you don't know *him*. He's more than the lies and the fear. And he's definitely not the one you should be after right now. You want to lock someone up? Then go find that freak who was trying to toss me into his van. Leave Ethan alone."

Victor sighed. "Like that, huh?"

Ethan stepped in front of her. "You don't understand the situation, so let me make things very clear to you, *agent*. No on hurts Carly. Not you. Not that bastard out there. You hunt him. You hunt him fast. Because if I find him first, there's not going to be anything left of him for you and your FBI team."

"Did you just threaten to kill a man?" Victor demanded. "Right in front of an FBI agent's face?"

Ethan laughed. "Sorry. My bad. I thought you realized I was a psychopath who didn't give a shit about anyone or anything. After all, that is what you were just telling Carly, right?"

Victor's eyes narrowed.

"Do your job. Find him. Or maybe *no one* will ever be seeing that asshole again." Then Ethan took Carly's hand. He started to lead her forward but a heavy rock pushed into the bottom of her foot, nearly piercing right through the soft sock, and Ethan immediately bent at her cry. He lifted her into his arms, holding her easily. "Don't worry, baby," Ethan assured her softly. "The car's waiting. We'll be home soon."

They'd taken five steps when Victor called out, "Never see him again, huh? Isn't that what happened to Quincy Atkins? He just disappeared, and no one ever saw him again. Seems like that might just be your MO, Barclay."

Ethan stopped.

"Don't," Carly whispered. "Let's just go. Take me home, Ethan."

They'd already moved away from the light, so she couldn't see Ethan's expression clearly. She wished that she could—she wanted to read the emotions that might be in his eyes.

After a moment, he kept walking. Unfortunately, Victor followed them. She saw Charles up ahead. He hurriedly opened the car door for her. Ethan bent and carefully put her in the backseat. His hands lingered on her as Victor's voice drifted in through that open door.

"Psychopath," he said. "That was *your* word. Ethan. But now that it's on the table...Ms. Shay, I hope you know that psychopaths don't feel much real emotion. They mimic. They show the world what they *think* others want to see. So if you believe you're seeing emotions from Ethan, if you think you've got him close to you, then you really need to think again. *I* can help you."

Ethan's hand slid over her cheek. "Be right back," he told her softly.

"Ethan—"

He slid away and a moment later, the car door slammed shut.

She inched forward, desperately trying to overhear the conversation going on outside, but, jeez, what had Ethan done? Totally sound-proofed his car?

***

Ethan smiled as he faced off against Agent Victor Monroe. They were both about the same height, even shared the same build. But that was where their similarities ended. This guy was the true blue agent type. A by-the-book mentality practically reeked from the guy.

He hadn't met Agent Monroe before seeing the guy in New York, but he'd heard of the man. A guy who was quickly moving up the FBI ranks.

A guy who was trouble.

"Why do you want me as an enemy?" Ethan asked him bluntly. "Because that is a seriously stupid move on your part."

Charles stood close by, trying to appear invisible, but also tense because—well, protecting Ethan's back was supposed to be his job.

"You're a criminal," Victor fired back. "My job is put guys like you away."

Ethan let his brows climb. "*Psychopaths* like me, right? Men who can't feel emotion. Men who are cold-blooded. Methodical. Men who commit terrible crimes, but always manage to keep their hands clean."

Victor inclined his head. "So you do know what you are."

Ethan smiled at him. "I also know what you are. I'm not the only one with secrets, and if you don't want your own life picked apart, then you shouldn't go nosing into my world." He glanced down at Victor's hands. "Interesting scars you've got there." Very, very faint...and old. Most people probably wouldn't have noticed them at all. Ethan noticed everything. "Not from a knife, not like my scars. Those you carry...you got those from beating the hell out of something, right?" *A very long time ago.*

The agent tensed. "Stay the hell out of my life."

"Only if you stay out of mine." He kept that cold smile in place. "Maybe I'm not the man you need to worry so much about."

"Because you've bought into legit businesses in the last few years?" Victor grunted. "Right, you think we didn't know all about that? Not just Ms. Shay's PR firm, but dozens of other companies. Clubs, bars, even tech companies. You sure do believe in branching out, don't you?"

Ethan shrugged.

"But I do wonder, where did you get all that start-up capital?"

"The hard way. I earned it." Through blood and sweat and hell. He knew the cops and the feds couldn't find anything wrong—not on paper—with his businesses. He'd made sure of it. "Don't know why you think I'm anything less than an honest man." He had no intention of ever seeing the inside of a prison. "Now, sorry to cut this shit short..." He wasn't sorry at all. "But Carly needs me."

He headed around to the other side of the car.

"I think a man like you is the last thing she needs." Victor's voice was somber. "And we *both* know that, don't we?"

Asshole. Ethan slid into the car. Automatically, his hand reached for Carly's. He might not be what Carly needed, but she sure as hell was exactly what he wanted.

And if that FBI agent persisted, then Ethan really would have to ruin that jerk's life.

***

She had both the FBI and Ethan Barclay at her beck and call. Again. Dammit.

Getting to her was going to be a challenge, but he wouldn't give up. One way or another, he'd have his time with Carly Shay. She might think that she was safe, using powerful men to shield herself, but it wasn't going to work.

Sooner or later, she'd be his.

The past had come calling. It was time for a reckoning.

Was she afraid? She really, really fucking should be. Enemies were closing in, and soon, even her allies wouldn't be able to protect her.

She'd be on her own.

And retribution would be at hand.

***

He'd actually brought her back to her apartment. She'd expected more of a fight from Ethan, but he just took her straight back home. Ethan accompanied her inside, searched the place thoroughly and—

"I'll set the alarm when you leave," Carly told him.

Ethan gave her an *Are-You-Serious* glance.

"Uh, yeah, I said I can set the alarm," she muttered as her toes curled into the hardwood floor. She'd ditched those crazy socks as soon as she was inside. Now she wanted to get rid of the scrubs and collapse into bed. The only problem with that plan was Ethan. And the fact that Ethan seemed to be lingering.

He headed to the door. Locked it. Set her alarm.

"How did you know my code?" she demanded, voice way too high.

He just tossed her a frown.

"Seriously, it's a legitimate question, Ethan. You can't just hack my system."

He turned fully toward her, crossed his arms over his chest, and stared her down. "I didn't hack your system, baby."

Why did he always have to use that
endearment with her? He didn't mean it. And it
was upsetting to her. Was he manipulating her, as
the agent had said? Playing some game?

I don't want to play.

"I saw you type in the code before," Ethan
added. "And it's not like I'd forget my own
birthday."

Shit. Had she seriously done that? Made her
security code his birthday? It hadn't been
deliberate, had it? Now her cheeks were stinging
and she just needed this day to end.

"You won't let me take you some place safe,
so I'm staying here with you."

She managed to stop her jaw from dropping.
Barely. "You aren't sleeping with me!"

"That's unfortunate. Because I've fantasized
about that plenty of times."

Her jaw dropped then. No help for it.

"But I didn't say I'd sleep with you. I said
stay. Just...*stay, baby.* Tonight, I'll bunk on the
couch."

"You don't have to do that! I'm fine here!"

His arms slid to his sides and he headed
toward her. She didn't back up but a nervous
energy flooded through her body. Then he was
right in front of her. His expression was
guarded—always, guarded—as he stared down at
her. "You're right. I don't have to do it."

Okay, so he'd leave.

"I *need* to stay. I need to know you're safe.
Because if I walk out that door tonight and leave

you on your own, I'll pretty much go fucking insane."

"Ethan..."

"Go crash in your room."

She didn't move.

"To be clear..." His voice roughened. "I want to touch you."

She wanted him to touch her. And she wanted him to leave. And she was a serious mess where he was concerned.

"But, I won't," Ethan said. "What I will do is stay out here, all night long. Anyone who comes for you, well, the SOB will have to go through me first."

Her heart had taken on the heavy tone of a drum beat in her ears. Agent Monroe had said that Ethan was mimicking emotions, but his eyes were so bright with feeling as he gazed down at her. In that second, she could read him—Need. Desire. Fury.

She eased out a slow breath. "I keep seeing that guy in my head. Coming at me with his knife. Telling me that he'd cut my throat if I made a sound."

Fury burned brighter in his stare.

Carly licked her lips as she came to a decision. "So, sure, you can stay on the couch. I'm not going to argue about that. I think I will sleep better with you here." *The devil you know...*

She turned away. The devil she knew was far better than the monster waiting in the dark.

"If you need me," his voice followed her. "Remember, I'm right here."

Oh, but he didn't understand. She'd always needed him. In one way or another. Resisting him, though, that had become a habit for her.

Was it time to break that habit?

***

Victor Monroe stared at the man in front of him. Dr. Keith Nelson was sweating. A little line of sweat ran over his upper lip. A bit of moisture wet his temples.

As Victor watched him, the guy took off his glasses and rubbed the lenses on his shirt. Talk about appearing nervous. You'd think the guy had never been called in for a talk with the FBI. Fear seemed to roll off the fellow.

But Victor knew better. This man—Dr. Nelson—had once treated some seriously dangerous patients. Patients that might even give Ethan Barclay a run for his money. So he didn't buy the nervous act. Though it did make him curious.

"I've told you before," Dr. Nelson said as he pushed his glasses back onto his nose. "I can't discuss my clients with you. It would be highly unethical."

Victor tapped his fingers on the table. They were in an interview room, courtesy of the local FBI. Victor had been called in on the Barclay/Shay case at the last minute. He really had more than enough shit to deal with at the moment. But when the Barclay case had tied in with one of his recent investigations, strings had been pulled. Victor had been reassigned.

And he'd found himself in New York, temporarily taking over a space at their FBI office. Even though his mind was somewhere else, on *someone* else.

Zoe.

But for the time being, he had to focus on this shit. As twisted as it all was. "A woman was attacked after leaving her session with you, doctor. In light of that situation, I'm sure you understand *why* you were called in."

Behind the lenses of his glasses, the doctor's eyes widened. "You haven't told me how Carly is doing."

There was such familiarity in the guy's voice when he talked about Carly Shay. Was their relationship professional? Personal? Both? He'd certainly not pegged Ethan Barclay for the sharing type.

"Ms. Shay was taken home by her friend." Deliberately, he paused. "Perhaps you know him? Ethan. Ethan Barclay?"

He saw the doctor's eyelids flicker. Had fear stolen across the man's face? For an instant, Victor thought that it had.

"He's about my height, maybe two hundred pounds. Dark hair." The doctor tensed more with every word. "Got some scars on his cheeks. Rather dangerous looking fellow."

Dr. Nelson licked his lips. "Is Carly okay?"

"Her injuries weren't severe," Victor said. "She was very lucky. Unfortunately, her attacker is still on the loose." And that pissed him off. He didn't like it when women were hurt—one of his hot button issues. The attacker's van had been found, ditched in another parking garage, but there had been no sign of the perp. Since he thought the guy was a professional, Victor was betting the van would wind up being a stolen vehicle, and he doubted any prints would be recovered.

"You'll catch him, won't you?" Dr. Nelson asked. He'd leaned forward in his chair.

"The local authorities are working on apprehending him." Victor always had to be careful when he moved in—the cops could be real territorial. The last thing he wanted was a pissing match that wound up hurting everyone. But he also wanted to find that perp and toss his ass in a cage. "But if you have information...if you know who might be threatening Ms. Shay, that intel could certainly prove useful. I understand that she's your patient and you have—"

"Not anymore." The response seemed to snap out from the shrink.

Victor lifted his brows. "Excuse me?"

"She terminated our sessions. A mistake. But she wouldn't listen." He gave a curt nod. "Tonight was our last meeting. I-I can't discuss her case, but she isn't my client any longer."

Interesting. Had Ethan Barclay been involved in that decision? Was he the reason Carly terminated her sessions? "Ethan was never your client."

A sharp shake of Nelson's head. "Don't really know him." His lips thinned. "Just saw him holding Carly before her appointment. She should know it's a mistake for her to get involved in a relationship with someone like him after what—" His eyes widened. He stopped. "I'm not talking to you any longer. It's late. My mind isn't working properly, and I will *not* violate privilege this way."

Why was Carly Shay seeing this shrink? Why did the guy think it was so bad for her to have a relationship? A cold knot formed in Victor's stomach as he began to piece together the past. Quincy Atkins had enjoyed hurting women. A few women had even mysteriously left D.C. after being spotted with him.

Left...*or been killed?*

Quincy hadn't been the only one to vanish. Victor knew because he'd poured over every file and every bit of data he could possibly find on the guy. The D.C. police had suspected that Quincy might be tied to the disappearance of a few girls who'd danced at his club.

The three women who'd vanished had been young. Runaways who'd grown up on the streets. According to the files he'd read, they'd all last been seen at one of Quincy's clubs. Friends had reported them missing. The D.C. cops had suspected Quincy but...

But nothing happened.

Then a few weeks later, according to those files, Quincy had disappeared.

Victor's fingers stopped drumming on the table. "You don't like Ethan Barclay, do you?"

"I don't know him." Dr. Nelson stood. "I have to go—"

"He's suspected of being one of the most influential crime bosses on the East Coast. The FBI has been trying to bust him for years, but he always gets away, scot-free."

Dr. Nelson paled.

"You treated plenty of criminals before, didn't you, doctor? You were on staff at Falling Waters State Hospital, a facility for the criminally insane, right after you got your license, correct?"

"I did my internship there." Dr. Nelson's response was hesitant. "Then I stayed on for a...a bit. It was important to understand the workings of...of a disturbed mind."

Disturbed. Interesting word choice. "You worked with sociopaths. Psychopaths. You—"

"Not all psychopaths or sociopaths are a threat to society." Now. Dr. Nelson had straightened his shoulders. "Many are perfectly functioning, normal people. Perhaps psychopaths don't feel what you think of as 'normal' emotional connections, but they are intelligent. Highly so. They're assertive, ruthless, determined. They can make for great CEOs or—"

"Doctors," Victor murmured when the other man broke off. "I've heard they make for great doctors."

Dr. Nelson cleared his throat. "A lack of empathy could be beneficial to a certain extent, say for a trauma surgeon who has to divorce himself from the emotions of the job in order to save a patient."

Victor smiled at him. "You went to med school. Did you ever have to divorce yourself from emotions?"

Dr. Nelson pushed his glasses up once more. "I'm not a threat here. I certainly didn't attack Carly!" He marched for the door. "We're done. If you have any other questions for me, then contact my attorney."

The door slammed after him, and Victor's smile slowly faded away.

CHAPTER FIVE

The bedroom door creaked open. The faintest pad of footsteps reached his ears. Ethan was lying on the couch, in pretty much one of the most uncomfortable positions he'd ever known, and when he heard Carly's approach, he immediately shot off the cushions and to his feet. "What's happening?" Ethan demanded as he closed in on her. He'd shut off the lights in the den, but his eyes had adjusted to the darkness and he could make out her form. "What's wrong?"

Before he reached her, Carly reached out and turned on a nearby lamp. A soft pool of light filled the area, and he saw that she was wearing an old t-shirt and a pair of loose shorts, shorts that exposed the wonderful, long expanse of her legs.

His cock surged at the sight of her. *Down, boy. Down fucking now.*

"The couch isn't comfortable for you. You're probably nearly twice its size."

"I've been on worse." Once upon a time, he'd even slept on the streets. Not a memory that he particularly enjoyed, but shit like that had made him into the man he was.

"I have plenty of room in my bed."

He shook his head, an instinctive move because she could *not* have just said that to him. No way. But his twitching cock was saying that, hell, yes, she'd just invited him to climb in bed with her. "Bad idea." Very, very bad.

"Why?"

What? Seriously? "Because if I get in that bed, I'll want to fuck you." And after the hell she'd been through already, the last thing she probably wanted was him pouncing on her like a starving man.

I've been desperate for her for years.

Her hand lifted and she—she touched his chest. He'd stripped off his shirt but kept on his jeans while trying to get comfortable on the couch. Now her fingers were lightly tracing his scars, and his whole body tensed at her touch.

His hand flew up and his fingers locked around her wrist. "You don't want to do that."

She looked up at him, her lashes slowly rising. "I do. I thought about this in my room. Thought about you because I couldn't sleep, and I realized—I do want this. I want you."

"Carly—"

"The truth is that I'd like to do all kinds of things...with you."

His eyes closed. "Ten seconds. I can give you ten seconds to get back in that room." Before his good intentions flew to hell. It wasn't as if he were used to good intentions, anyway, and for her to admit that she wanted him that way...*too much*. His control started to shred. A woman like her—

she needed control. She needed care. She needed a fucking prince charming.

She was about to get the devil himself.

"I've had other lovers. I didn't—I didn't lock myself away because of what happened."

His gaze lifted to hold hers.

"I wasn't going to let Quincy take away my life." She licked her lower lip, a quick swipe of her tongue. "But it wasn't easy. Actually, it was so hard that I thought it would destroy me—just making love. Just letting down my guard enough for someone else to get close."

She was destroying him right then. One word, one breath, at a time.

"I never wanted anyone else, though," Carly continued, voice husky, "not the way I want you, Ethan. You make me ache from just a touch while other men...I still flinch away from them. I have to school myself. I have to fight my fears with them. But with you, there isn't anything to fight. There's just this need I have. Maybe it's because I knew you before. Maybe it's because you were there...then. Because you know everything and I don't have to pretend." She drew in a shuddering breath. "Or maybe the why just doesn't matter at all. Maybe I just want you, and you—I know you want me, too."

His thumb was caressing her inner wrist.

"I'm not asking for some kind of promise here." She inched closer to him. "I'm talking about one night. Me and you. I want you...you want me. Why not see what it would be like?" Her laughter was bitter. "Or maybe I'll stop you in the middle of the whole damn thing. I've done that before. When *he* gets in my mind."

His heart burned. Carefully, he released her wrist. Then his hands rose and slid under her delicate jaw. He tipped back her head and leaned forward to kiss her. His lips pressed to hers. Slow. Tender. And he kept a stranglehold on his control.

That control *wouldn't* be breaking. Not with her. No matter what he had to do, he'd keep it in place with Carly.

He licked her lower lip, then sucked it lightly. When he eased back, just a bare inch, Ethan promised, "There will be no one in your mind but me. Tonight, I swear, it's just us." He would give her as much pleasure as she could stand. All damn night long. Until she told him to stop.

He'd give her anything. He wasn't going to walk away from her. He'd dreamed of Carly wanting him, too many times. This wasn't a dream. And he wasn't a fool.

She caught his hand in hers and walked back with him into her bedroom. The bedroom smelled like her. Sweet, sensual. A light, floral scent hung in the air. Her bed covers had been pushed back, and the brass-bed waited for them. She started to lead him to the bed.

He stopped. "There are going to be a few rules first." His voice came out too hard, but a sharp tide of lust would do that to a man. Make him sound more like a desperate beast.

She turned back toward him.

"First...if anything scares you, you tell me to fucking stop, got it? I don't care how far gone I may seem, you say stop, and I freeze." They had to be clear on that.

"S-should we use some kind of safe word?"

Okay, he just had to kiss her again because she said that with her voice trembling. A harder, deeper kiss. "We don't need one, baby. Stop is all you have to say." Stop—and he'd barely breathe. Because this mattered. She mattered.

Carly needed to know that. This wasn't some bedroom game. This was him. Her. No fantasy but a sexy, consuming reality that might drive him to the edge—but he would not let it take him beyond.

"Rule two..." His voice was growing more ragged by the moment. "When we actually get ready to fuck, you're on top."

Her gaze flickered and he was sure that he saw the flash of relief in her gaze. He was trying to set up this scene so that nothing would remind her of the past—or of that bastard Quincy.

"You control the pleasure," he said. "Because rule three is that you have to tell me *exactly* what you like...and what you don't."

She nodded. "But only if we follow rule four..."

He'd stepped toward her, intent on stripping that t-shirt off her, but at those words, Ethan hesitated. "Rule four?"

"You tell me *exactly* what you like...and what you don't. Because I want to give you pleasure, Ethan."

She pretty much gave him pleasure just by breathing, but he wasn't going to say that. Not right then. She didn't realize just what she was getting into with him. There would be plenty of time for that discovery, later.

His hands lifted toward her. He caught the hem of her t-shirt and lifted it over her head, being extra careful not to disturb the small, white bandage near her collarbone. Then he dropped her shirt to the floor as he stared at her breasts. Beautiful. Full. With dark, tight nipples. He wanted to touch those nipples, but not with his hands.

He wrapped his hands around her waist and he lifted her up, holding her easily even as her hands flew out and locked around his shoulders. Then he put his mouth on her nipple. Licked and sucked and she tasted even sweeter than he'd imagined. Sweet and perfect, like she'd been made just for him.

He sucked, harder, as the desire pulsed inside of him. She wasn't trying to pull away. Carly arched against his mouth, offering more of herself to him. Hell, yes. He kissed his way to her other breast. He licked that nipple, kissed her sweet flesh. Then drew her nipple into his mouth.

"*Ethan!*" She'd never said his name quite that way before.

He liked that demand.

He didn't let her go, not yet. He savored her taste. He made sure that he licked and sucked and kissed until she was shaking in his arms.

Then, slowly, he slid her back down until her toes touched the floor. His cock shoved hard against the front of his jeans, so there was no way Carly could miss his desire for her.

She didn't pull away from him. Her hands stayed locked around his shoulders. Her gaze met his.

"Are you wet for me, yet?" Ethan asked.

A shiver slid over her.

"Let's find out," Ethan said. His hands caught her shorts and he pushed them down her body. When he saw that she wasn't wearing any panties...

Fuck, fuck, fuck me!

He didn't move for a moment as he made sure that his control would hold. *Don't pounce. Don't rush. Give her time. Give her everything.*

His fingers slid down her stomach, down, on down until he reached the apex of her thighs. Her legs were braced apart, and it was so easy for him to slip two fingers up into her sensitive core.

She was warm. She was wet. But not wet enough.

"Sit on the bed, baby."

She did, her movements a bit jerky.

He didn't follow her on the bed. He didn't want to do anything that would put his body on top of hers, didn't want to make any move that might make her feel trapped or overwhelmed.

He was used to dominant sex. He liked dominant sex. Hard and rough and dirty.

But this was different. This was Carly. And he would have sooner cut off his own damn arm than scare her.

So he sank to his knees beside the bed. He positioned his body between her legs, and he locked his hands around her waist as he pulled her forward, positioning her at the edge of the mattress. Then he eased her legs apart, opening her even more. Making sure that she was fully exposed to him.

Such a gorgeous, pink treat.

"Scream if you want," he said. "But I've just got to see..."

"See what?" She was balanced on her elbows, craning up to see him.

"I've got to see what you taste like when you come."

Then he put his mouth on her. She tensed immediately, and her thighs tried to close, but she hadn't said that magic word yet, and he worked her gently. Licking. Caressing. Using his fingers and his tongue, and her taste had him feeling drunk—*so good*—but he wasn't stopping. Not now. No way.

He found the center of her desire. He stroked and he licked, and he pushed his index finger deep into her. She fell back on the bed, and when he glanced up at her, he saw that she'd fisted the sheets in her hands.

Good. Not good enough. Had she forgotten the all-important rule number three? He pulled away from her.

"Ethan!" An immediate cry of protest.

"You have to tell me what you like."

Her breath was heaving out. "What you were doing. I liked it—a lot!"

He smiled. "What part, baby? Tell me...do you want my fingers on you? In you?"

"Yes! Yes, I-I want your fingers in me."

"And..." He needed her to say it. Needed those words so he'd know that she was with him for every single moment.

"And I want your mouth on me. *Please, Ethan...I was so close.* Closer than I've ever been."

Her words pierced right to his heart. *Closer than I've ever been.* Shit, did that mean she hadn't climaxed before? Oh, hell, no, but she deserved pleasure. He'd make her climax until she went wild.

Once wouldn't be enough.

Not for her. Not for him.

He pushed his fingers back into her—not one, but two this time, and he loved the way she gasped and arched her hips up to him. Then he put his mouth on her. Licking and sucking and not stopping, not when he felt her tense up, not when her hips were riding his fingers. He thrust his hand against her, then he pulled his fingers out, and he put his tongue into—

She tasted like heaven when she came.

She was chanting his name. Music to his ears.

It was easy enough to keep her climax going. Her legs were shaking. Her cheeks were flushed. She was absolutely delectable. He kept licking her.

He licked her straight into a second orgasm.

When the final shudders slid from her body, he eased back enough to stare at her. He licked his lips, savoring her taste, and knew that he'd always crave more.

But maybe she wanted him to stop now. They were back to rule number three. She had to tell him, exactly, what she wanted.

She pushed up to her elbows again. Her nipples were tight and tempting and he wanted to suck them again.

He actually wanted to kiss her—every single inch of her body.

"Will it feel like that...when you...when your cock is in me?"

He already had precum on his cock. "Ready to find out?"

She gave a nod.

He shook his head. "The words, baby. The words."

Carly sucked in a sharp breath. "I want you, in me. *You.*"

Hell, yes. There was no other place that he wanted to be more. Ethan rose to his feet. He took his wallet from his back pocket. It was a damned good thing he was prepared because walking away from her would have ripped out his guts. He ditched his pants.

Her gaze slid over his body.

He put the condom on, rolling it over his erection, then he moved toward her.

Carly tensed.

"It's okay, baby." He fought to keep his voice sounding easy. Not demanding. Not animal-like. *I feel like a fucking beast right now. Want her too much.* "You're calling the shots, remember? And it's all about pleasure, for us both."

She scooted back a bit. Most people he knew—his enemies—said he didn't have a heart. That he'd lost it and what remained of his soul long ago, but when Carly scooted back, it sure as hell felt like someone had taken a knife to his chest...and that knife was sliding right into his heart.

He lay down on the bed. "Climb on top." He figured that position would reassure her the most. Slowly, hesitantly, she did. Her knees pushed into the mattress on either side of his body, and her silken thighs slid over his hips.

"Now you do it," Ethan told her. *Control. Control. Control.* Sweat was breaking out on his body as he fought to lock his muscles and hold the fuck still. "Guide me inside."

Her fingers curled around his shaft.

His back teeth ground together.

She rose up, and then she slid his cock toward the entrance of her body. Because she was so wet and ready—he'd made sure of it—he slid right inside of her as she arched down against him.

She gasped.

His eyes squeezed shut. *Control.* She was freaking heaven around him. Hot and tight and better than he'd dreamed. Yeah, he'd had plenty of dreams about her over the years. Dreams didn't even touch reality.

"You feel good," Carly whispered.

She felt fucking fantastic.

"Can I...move now?"

He cracked open his eyes. "I'm yours. Do whatever the hell you want." She probably didn't get just how true those words were.

She lifted up, then pushed back down. Her movements were slow at first, tentative. Then she went faster. Harder. The back of his feet shoved into the mattress and his fingers flew up and locked around her hips. He wanted more, so much—

"Ethan?"

His hands jerked away from her and he grabbed the sheets around them. He fisted them, holding tight. If she said stop...

"I like...the way you feel...Ethan...So much..." Then she was moving again. Fast and hot and wild, and his hips slammed up against her because Carly's rhythm was frantic and perfect. Just the way he'd wanted her. Out of control and desperate for release. No fear. No pain. Nothing at all there but the two of them and the pleasure they gave each other.

She came first. He felt her delicate inner muscles squeeze around him as Carly choked out a little scream that he would never forget. Her body sagged forward and his hands flew up, locking tightly around her.

And then he kept thrusting, loving the feel of her orgasm squeezing around him, and when his release hit him...

Hell, yes. The pleasure ripped through him with enough force to take his breath. Again and again that hard, rough wave seemed to batter him, and it was fucking insane. Too good.

The best of his life.

She was the best.

And when his thundering heartbeat filled his ears, when he heard the rough rasp of his breath, Ethan realized just how far gone he was.

Can't let her go now. Can't ever let go.

***

Keith Nelson unlocked the door to his apartment, a fancy piece on the West Side that had been in the family for years. He'd almost lost it a few years back, but luckily, his private practice had started to pay off. The place was his sanctuary now, his escape when he needed to step back from the world and the darkness that could linger there.

He flipped on the light switch.

"Hello, doctor…"

A man was sitting in his favorite leather chair, sprawling there as if he owned the place. *He doesn't. I do.* Blood and sweat had paid for that place, no matter what others might think.

But Keith didn't let his fear show as he squared his shoulders and faced the man in that chair. It wasn't the first time he'd come home to find an intruder waiting for him. An overzealous patient had snuck in before, and Keith had dealt with the man.

When mental illness was your life, you learned very, very quickly, how to handle the deranged.

"You don't look surprised to find me here," the man continued. The light glinted off his dark blond hair.

Did the guy have a weapon? Keith didn't. He used to carry pepper spray with him, but now that his patients were the non-violent sort—for the most part—he'd felt safer. Safe enough to travel without any sort of weapon.

The man rose. His jacket eased back just a bit, and Keith saw the holster there. *Gun.*

His mouth went dry.

"I have some questions about one of your patients," the blond man said as he closed in on Keith. "And you are going to tell me every single thing that I need to know..."

***

Someone was pounding on the door. Ethan cracked open one eye and growled. He was comfortable. Carly was on top of him, she was soft and smelled so sweet, and the last thing he wanted to do was move.

But someone was still pounding. Hell.

"Ethan?" Now Carly was awake. And that meant that she'd move away.

Whoever was doing that pounding had just made Ethan's shit list.

"What's going on?" She blinked a bit blearily at him. Faint rays of light drifted through the blinds. Day had come. Day and, no doubt, more trouble.

"You stay here," he told her. "I'll go find out."

But the sleepiness was already fading from her eyes as full awareness flooded back. She looked down at her body, realized she was naked, and hurriedly jumped from the bed, dragging the sheet with her.

Unfortunate.

"I'm not just staying here!" She'd rushed to the closet and was dressing frantically. "It's my house. My door! I'm going to see what is happening."

And she was kind of like a whirlwind as she dressed at a rapid-fire speed. He made a mental note. Carly was not into pillow talk. Then Ethan grabbed his jeans and yanked them on. He didn't bother putting on a shirt because Carly was already rushing down the hallway.

He followed a few paces behind her, and then he saw her put her eye to her peephole. "It's the FBI agent," she said, her voice hushed. "Again."

Agent Monroe was getting on his nerves.

She looked over her shoulder at him. "Charles is out there, too."

The door pounded again. "Ms. Shay!" A male voice called. No doubt, Victor Monroe's voice. "Open up! The last thing you want is this conversation happening out here for all your neighbors to hear."

She yanked open the door. "I figure my neighbors can already hear plenty." She glowered at him. "And actually, just so you know, the one across the hall isn't even here. She's been out of the country for weeks."

Ethan closed in, slowly. Charles met his gaze and gave an apologetic shrug. "Saw him coming in, boss," Charles said.

He'd stationed Charles as a watcher outside the building. Only Charles should have *called* him and given him a head's up on the situation. Not let the FBI get so close.

"He moved fast," Charles added, "so I figured I'd follow him up."

Right.

"What's happening?" Carly demanded. "Why are you here?" She backed up until her shoulders hit Ethan's chest.

He liked that she'd moved closer to him. He hoped that she knew he would always have her back. Always.

"The local cops got a call about two hours ago," Victor announced. "Seems that a neighbor of Dr. Nelson's got worried. She went to take her dog out and saw that his door was wide open. When the cops went inside, they found signs of a struggle, and the good doctor, well, he seems to have vanished."

"What?" Carly demanded.

Ethan's lips twisted. "Let me guess. You think I had something to do with his disappearance?"

But the FBI agent shook his head. "Actually, I don't. At least, not directly. We had eyes on you, so we know that *you* didn't leave this apartment. Now, do I think you hired someone to attack him? Maybe. But my instincts say someone else took him. Someone who wanted to know just what Ms. Shay had confessed during her sessions with him."

"The man who attacked me in the parking garage," Carly said.

Victor nodded. "It's possible that you weren't even his original target yesterday. The duct tape, the rope, the handcuffs? All waiting in the parking garage? *You* weren't even supposed to come out that way, but Dr. Nelson was. Maybe the attacker just took you because the opportunity presented itself. Nelson could have been the abduction target all along. After all, he's the weak link. No protection. No Ethan Barclay threatening to destroy anyone who gets close to him."

Ah, so Victor had heard about the orders Ethan had put out. He'd let it be known—loud and clear—that anyone coming after Carly would have to deal with *him*.

Victor put his hands on his hips. "So now Ms. Shay, the danger around you is going to mount even more. Dr. Nelson didn't tell me anything. He held onto the old patient/doctor confidentiality bit, but how long do you think that attitude is going to last if he's being tortured? Don't you think all of your secrets will be coming out of him...sooner or later?"

Carly didn't speak.

Anger flashed on Victor's face. "Dammit, a man's life is at stake here! You need to help—"

"Dr. Nelson can't tell what he doesn't know." Her voice was low. "I've always been very careful with my shrinks. They know I was raped—"

Victor's face tensed.

"But they don't know what else happened." Her hand caught Ethan's. "Some things, no one else knows."

"Enough," Ethan snarled. "Get the fuck out of her hallway and come inside. You want to question us, fine, then do it. But you aren't putting her pain on display for the world to see." Her courage was humbling him. She'd always done that, though. *Fucking humbled me.*

Did she realize it?

Victor came inside. Charles followed him. Ethan made sure the door was shut and the alarm reset.

"How can I help Dr. Nelson?" Carly asked. "Because I don't want him suffering for me. I don't want that happening to anyone."

Victor nodded. "Then I need a list, Ms. Shay. I need a list of the people who might be gunning for you. I need to know who would be so desperate that he'd abduct a shrink, just because he wanted to know your secrets."

But it wasn't really Carly's secrets that Ethan believed the attacker wanted. "There's one man you need to be investigating." His smile was bitter. "I mean, investigating more than me." Because he'd known he was on the FBI's radar for years. "Curtis Thatch is the man you need to be looking at..."

He saw recognition flare in Monroe's eyes.

"That's right," Ethan told him. "Quincy's younger brother." One who had smartly changed his last name so as not to be painted by that infamous brush. "Sometimes, families can be fucking killer." Ethan knew that with utter certainty. "You think the psycho apple fell far from the tree? Just because Curtis got himself an MD and a job in a fancy hospital? Think again. The need for revenge can lurk in a man's heart for years, and when the opportunity presents itself..." He smiled. "Vengeance erupts."

CHAPTER SIX

The club was dark. Cavernous. Carly stood in the middle of the place as the lights flashed on all around her. *Reflections.* The new club that she was supposed to be promoting. Ethan's club.

They were alone in that club, and she should have felt safe.

She didn't.

Agent Monroe had revealed to her and Ethan that Curtis Thatch had taken a sabbatical from his job as a trauma surgeon at Glenlake Hospital in upstate New York. None of his acquaintances seemed to know exactly where Curtis had gone. He'd locked up his house and headed out.

Five days ago.

"We don't have to do this now," Ethan said as he strode from the back. The bar gleamed to his left. A long, marble bar that she could easily imagine packed with men and women on opening night. "Trust me, this shit can wait."

But Carly shook her head. "Trust me, waiting is the last shit I want to do."

His lips quirked.

"I need to stay busy. If I'm not busy, then I'm just thinking—again and again—about Dr. Nelson."

"The guy is a prick, Carly."

"Whatever he is—he doesn't deserve to be tortured." And she kept seeing that in her head. Him, being handcuffed. Threatened. Killed? "I never told any of my shrinks specifics. It seemed safer that way. None of them can give up info on me." But now she wondered—were the others at risk, too? Was everyone she'd come in contact with over the years in danger? Her breath caught as she had that thought and Carly surged across the club toward Ethan. She grabbed his arm. "My sister! Julianna, she's—"

"Safe, Carly. Julianna is totally safe. Did you forget, her new lover happens to own his own bodyguard business? I briefed Devlin on the threat before I left D.C. There's no way he will let anyone get close to her."

Her breath eased out, but her heartbeat didn't slow down.

"Nothing will happen to her. I promise you that."

Julianna was her step-sister, and she was the only family that Carly had. Carly's mother had died when she was a baby and her father—he'd finally drank himself to death years ago. Literally right after her nightmare with Quincy. She'd needed her father to be there for her. Needed it so much.

But he'd been in a bottle instead. And then he'd just been—dead. Only a few days after her time in hell with Quincy.

Rely on yourself, Carly. Trust yourself. Everyone else lets you down. But...Julianna hadn't let her down. Carly had learned—too late—that her sister had paid a terrible price for Carly's crimes. She wouldn't let Julianna suffer again.

"Do you have your men searching for Dr. Nelson?" She suspected that he did, and she needed to know the truth. She just didn't know how much information it was safe for her to ask about. Before, he'd worried about listening devices at her apartment, but what about this club? Since it hadn't officially opened yet and access to the place had been limited, did that mean it was safer than her home?

Or was the FBI already monitoring every single inch of Reflections?

"I have teams looking for him," Ethan said.

That was good to know.

"And teams are also looking for Curtis."

The name made her tense as she eased away from Ethan. "Have you met him?"

"Years ago. On the second anniversary of his brother's disappearance, he came to see me."

That was scary. "What did you tell him?"

"I didn't tell him anything, not at first. He told me that he'd make me pay. That he figured I was the one behind Quincy's disappearance."

She paced a few feet away. Her hand touched the top of the bar. The surface felt cold to her.

"I told the guy he needed to wake up and smell the damn coffee. He was acting as if Quincy was some noble hero, when the world knew what a piece of shit he was. I asked Curtis if his life was better or worse without his big brother..."

She glanced back at him. "What did he say?"

"He left. I didn't hear from him again, not directly, not until Duvato started trying to make deals with the FBI."

Carly absorbed that information for a moment, then said, "But Curtis isn't part of his brother's criminal group, right? I mean, that gang is all gone now." She hoped. "And you said he was a doctor—"

"I don't know exactly *what* Curtis is. But I will."

She had no doubt that he'd learn plenty. Her gaze returned to the bar. *Focus on business. Stop being so afraid.* "We'll, ah, we'll get promos going on all the major TV and radio stations and we'll make sure that people understand opening night is—"

"Are we going to talk about it?"

Her shoulders tensed. "It?" She looked into the mirror that waited a few feet away. People who came to the bar would see their reflections in that mirror as they drank and partied. The mirror served to make the club look even bigger on the inside—actually, there were mirrors everywhere. That was where the name came from.

Reflections.

On the ceiling. On the walls. Mirrors nearly enclosed the club.

She stared at her reflection and saw a pale woman, one who had eyes that seemed too big. Ethan walked up behind her. Dark and dangerous Ethan. Handsome in such a killer way.

"*It*," he said again. He didn't touch her. "You know, the awesome sex we had last night."

Her lips curled. "It was pretty awesome." Amazing. And she hadn't been afraid, not with him. He'd been right—it had just been her and him. No ghosts.

"Don't overwhelm my ego." His head inclined.

Laughter slipped from her. "I don't think your ego has any problems. I don't—" She broke off because his expression had altered so completely. Hardened—nearly turning to stone. She whirled toward him, alarm flaring in her. "Ethan?"

He caught her around the waist and lifted her up, sitting her on that bar. Then he moved his hands away from her, fast, almost as if he didn't trust himself to touch her. He slapped his hands down on either side of her body. "You haven't done that in a long time."

"Done what?"

"Really *laughed*." He cleared his throat and said, "I think I'd forgotten what your laugh sounded like."

Her hands rose and settled along his shoulders. "And I can't remember the last time I heard you laugh, and honestly mean the sound."

"My life isn't about laughter."

"Then what's it about?"

"Being a tough SOB. Staying two steps ahead of the competition. Showing no weakness." He shook his head. "But I screwed up."

"How?"

"You." His golden gaze seemed to bore right into her. "You're my weak spot, and I think too many people know it."

"Ethan—"

The lights that he'd turned on suddenly flashed off. She tensed, but didn't cry out. The building had recently been renovated. A few lighting issues should be expected. Typical. Nothing to worry about.

Right?

Then her phone rang, vibrating in her pocket. The vibration made her jump.

The club wasn't in total darkness. It was daylight outside, so she could still see fairly well, since some of the sunlight trickled inside Reflections, but unease slithered through her.

"The breaker," Ethan said. "I'll go check it."

Her phone kept ringing. Was it so wrong that she wanted to grab him and say that she'd come with him? *He's just checking the breaker. Relax.*

When he moved back, she jumped from the bar and pulled her phone from the pocket. But when she saw the caller ID on the screen, shock and relief rocked through her. "Dr. Nelson!"

Ethan froze, just a few steps away.

She put the phone to her ear. "Dr. Nelson! Where are you? Where—"

"He's...coming for you..." Static crackled on the line. "Get...out..."

Get out? "Where are you? The FBI is searching for you!"

"Bomb...wants to take out you...and Ethan...knows..."

That one word went straight through her. *Bomb*. "Ethan." The phone nearly fell from her hand as she stared at him. "Bomb. Nelson says there is a bomb!"

But where was the bomb? At her apartment? At the PR Firm?

Dear God...at Reflections?

"Get out..." Nelson's words were a rough tangle of sound in her ear. "Of...club..."

How did he even know she was in the club?

But Ethan was grabbing her hand and pulling her toward the front door. She ran with him, desperate to escape. If a bomb was inside, just how much time did they have? Carly feared the explosion would go off at any moment, rocking the building and killing them both.

Ethan shoved open the door. He pushed her out front, then followed but—

A man was in her path. A man with blond hair and green eyes. Eyes that were familiar to her.

Those eyes widened when he saw her. "Ms. Shay. We need to talk."

He needed to get out of her way. They all had to get out of there.

"You don't know me," the guy continued, side-stepping when she tried to get around him. "But I'm Curtis Thatch. And—"

He didn't get to say anymore. Because Ethan had just driven his fist into the guy's face. Curtis went down, slamming into the ground. And Ethan wrapped his arm around Carly's waist. "Move, move, *move...*"

Only he wasn't giving Carly the chance to move. He was carrying her and running and Curtis was stumbling after them.

Then Reflections exploded. She and Ethan hurtled toward the ground, and even when they hit, he was on top of her, shielding her with his body. She could feel the lance of fire against her skin, and for a moment, she stopped being able to hear anything at all. The *boom* had been so loud and the sudden silence after it was startling—no terrifying. At first, she feared that her ear drums had burst.

She could see Ethan above her. His mouth was moving. What was he saying? What—

"*—Baby, where are you hurt?*"

His voice hit her like a drum, each word pounding through her. Carly shook her head. She didn't feel particularly hurt. Maybe some bumps. Maybe some bruises, but she was okay. She hadn't burned alive so that was a serious win in her book.

Ethan rose slowly and pulled Carly to her feet. Her shoes crunched on something and when she looked down, she saw shattered pieces of glass littering the ground. Not just glass—*mirror*. Broken mirror chunks were everywhere. *So much more than seven years bad luck...*

"Is she hurt?"

Her head whipped to the left. Curtis Thatch was there. His clothes appeared ash-covered and blood dripped from a cut on his cheek. He started running toward her. "Is she okay?"

Before he could reach her, Ethan grabbed the other man. He shoved Curtis to the ground. "Stay the hell away from her!"

But Curtis didn't stay down. He surged right back to his feet. "I'm a doctor, dammit! I can help her!"

She didn't need help. Her ears were ringing, but she was fine. Her gaze slid to the burning building. So much for Ethan's new club, but at least they were okay. *Alive.*

Ethan caught her hand in his. His fingers threaded with hers. "We have to get out of the open...It's not safe like this."

But bystanders had gathered around them. A thick crowd, seeming to come from nowhere. A cop was there, too, trying to control the scene, but madness was taking over. So much madness.

A dark SUV slid to a stop near the curb. She wasn't surprised to see Agent Monroe leap from that vehicle. He rushed toward her and Ethan.

Another hand grabbed her, trying to yank her away from Ethan. She looked up and into Curtis's eyes. No wonder they'd seemed familiar. They were the same shade of green that Quincy's had been. For just a moment, past and present blurred for her. She screamed and kicked at him.

"No, no, I want to help you!" Curtis said. He swore and tightened his grip. "Let me—"

He didn't say anything else. Because Ethan attacked. Not just a punch this time. Not some shove. Ethan launched his body at the other man and tore into him with a fury. Violent. Hard. Primal. Again and again, Ethan slammed his fist into the other man.

Curtis didn't hit him back. Carly wasn't even sure if Curtis could fight.

"Ethan..." Carly barely whispered his name.

His head swung toward her.

And that was when Agent Monroe grabbed him. Victor yanked Ethan away from Curtis and pushed him to the side. Only Ethan didn't seem to realize that an FBI agent had grabbed him. He whirled and lunged right for Victor.

"No!" Carly cried. But it was too late. Ethan had driven his fist right at Victor. And blood had just poured from the agent's busted lip.

"That'll do it," Victor snarled. "Assaulting a federal officer. Ethan Barclay, I think your ass is finally getting locked up."

Carly glanced behind Ethan. Reflections was still burning. And the cops—they were all closing in. Not on her.

On Ethan.

***

Ethan was used to being inside an interrogation room. Over the years, he'd gotten plenty of interrogation experience. So he sat back and made himself comfortable as he waited. He glanced at his hands. His knuckles were red. Scratched. And he still smelled like fire and ash.

My club...destroyed.

But it had just been a building. Wood, bricks, and mirrors. Reflections could be replaced. If something had happened to Carly, if she'd been hurt—there would have been no replacing her.

The door opened. Agent Victor Fucking Monroe stood there. The guy looked cocky and arrogant. That wouldn't last long.

Ethan just lifted a brow as the other man approached him and sat down at the little table in the room.

"For someone who just committed a major screw-up," Victor drawled. "You don't look particularly concerned." He tilted his head to the side. "No lawyer?"

"Sophie is in D.C. If I need her, she'll be here immediately." But he didn't think he needed Sophie Sarantos, not just yet. He also didn't want to pull her into this mess, not until he figured out exactly what was happening. He and Sophie had been friends since they were kids, but the woman was happy now. All snug and in domestic bliss with her fierce bastard of a lover. While Ethan didn't always like the guy, he respected the hell out of Lex Jensen. Lex was fanatical about Sophie's safety, so if Victor called in his lawyer and Sophie came to New York, he knew that Lex would be in tow, too.

"Oh, I think you'll need her," Victor said. He touched his lip. Yeah, it was busted. So what? "You assaulted a federal officer, and I got about ten witnesses who say you also assaulted Curtis Thatch, when all the guy did was say he was a doctor who wanted to help."

Ethan laughed. "I don't believe in coincidences. They just don't happen."

A furrow appeared between Victor's eyebrows.

Did he really have to break this shit down? Fine. "My place explodes, and just who happens to be standing outside my door? Curtis Thatch. Standing there, just waiting for us to run right out after Dr. Nelson calls with his desperate warning..."

"We're still trying to locate Nelson," Victor said. "I've got techs trying to track his phone."

"Good for you," Ethan murmured.

Victor's blue eyes narrowed.

"Coincidences," Ethan continued, giving a shake of his head. "No, it wasn't by chance that Curtis was out there. He was waiting for us. Maybe he planted the bomb and he wanted to see for himself when Carly and I both were blown to hell. Maybe he's one of those hands-on types." He shrugged. "You're the FBI agent. You figure that crap out."

Victor leaned toward him. "You're right. I am the FBI agent. And I've definitely figured out one thing in particular. You're dangerous. Unstable. You can't be trusted to keep Carly Shay safe, and I think you're a threat to everyone you meet."

Which meant the guy wasn't going to let him walk out of that building anytime soon.

Unless...

"Coincidences," Ethan murmured. Then he said one name. "Zoe."

Victor's eyelids flickered. "Excuse me?"

Ethan glanced around the little room. "Where is the surveillance equipment in this place? I'm sure it's turned on. I'd hate for there to be some kind of malfunction." Then he glanced back at the FBI agent and just waited.

He was gambling here, but his recent investigation on Victor Monroe had turned up a few interesting facts.

And a very useful link that led from Victor right back to...*me*. Coincidence? Hell, no.

A muscle jerked in Victor's jaw, then he pushed away from the table. He left the room without another word. Ethan leaned back a bit in his chair, lifting up the front two legs as he waited, waited...

A few moments later, Victor was back. Only the guy looked seriously pissed. Ethan pushed his chair forward, bringing the legs back down.

Victor grabbed his chair and leaned over him. "You fucking sonofabitch..." Victor snapped at him. "What the hell do you know about Zoe?"

Bingo.

"I'm guessing you turned off the cameras and the sound recording equipment, huh?" Ethan murmured.

"I will destroy you."

Promises, promises. He tried to look shocked. "Is that any way for an FBI agent to talk?"

Victor growled.

"Zoe Peters," Ethan said. "A beautiful woman. Incredible dancer. She actually used to work at one of my places in Vegas. *Not* as a stripper," he hurried to say when Victor's eyes went feral, "but as a showgirl. She's got some moves you wouldn't believe."

"I could kill you right now and say you tried to escape."

Maybe. "That's not who you are." He might actually have just found an agent he could trust.

"You don't know anything about—"

"I got this cop friend in D.C." Since there were no cameras going, he felt safe in revealing this. "You would not believe the connections that woman has." Faith Chestang could always manage to surprise him. And to think, when they'd first met, she'd been so ready to lock him away. Oh, but how times could change. "She tapped into your FBI file, pulling some strings that came in mighty handy."

Victor's face was a mask of hate.

"I know you worked the Luther Bates case." Talk about a twisted freak. Luther Bates had given new meaning to the word *sadistic*. The guy put out hits on everyone who got in his way. Luckily for the rest of the world, Luther was currently rotting in a maximum security prison. The FBI was chomping at the bit to get Luther to talk to them, but so far, he seemed to be staying quiet.

The FBI kept trying, though. And the FBI agent who'd gone to visit dear twisted Luther the most over the last few weeks?

Special Agent Victor Monroe.

Only Victor had taken that intense interest in the guy *after* Zoe Peters had vanished. Ah, Zoe. A woman with a past she wanted dead and buried.

Since Zoe had vanished a few weeks ago, most folks thought *she* was dead.

Ethan wasn't most folks. "I also know," he said softly, "that you helped Zoe to disappear."

Victor straightened immediately. "Don't know what the hell you're talking about."

"Really?" He'd put the pieces together himself. With intel from Faith...and Zoe. "That's not the impression Zoe gave me. She actually thought she could trust you."

And, just like that, all emotion vanished from Victor's face.

"Didn't I mention that she called me recently? She needed money, and I was someone she thought she could count on."

Victor shook his head.

"I sent her the cash, and now, I know exactly where she is."

Victor's hand slammed down on the table. "You're threatening this woman? This Zoe?"

Ethan rolled his eyes. "Don't act like there isn't a personal involvement between you two. You're the rule following agent, but you broke every rule..." His head cocked to the right as he studied his prey. "In order to protect the daughter of a sadistic piece of shit like Bates."

Victor's eyes widened, just for a moment.

That's right. I know who her daddy is.

Victor sucked in a sharp breath. "You think you're blackmailing me?"

Blackmail was such an ugly word. "We both have people that we want to keep safe. You want Zoe to stay off the radar, and I—I want to make sure that no threats come close to Carly."

"You'd risk a woman's life..."

"Actually, *you're* the one putting Zoe at risk. The FBI has trouble in its ranks, and that trouble...it's going to raise its head again soon. *You're* being watched, Agent Monroe. Other people either know of your connection to Zoe or they damn well suspect it. And if you're not careful, you'll wind up killing the one woman you want to protect."

Victor shook his head. "You—"

"I can help you," Ethan offered.

Victor's eyes turned to slits. His cheeks had flushed an angry red.

"I can get some of the heat taken off Zoe. I can put out the word that I know where her body is. All the enemies that Bates has—they'd back off. A dead woman isn't worth their time."

Silence.

"But I can't do that shit while I'm locked up in here," Ethan continued. He gave the agent a grim smile. "So maybe go pull some strings...*and get my ass out of this place!*"

***

He was watching her. She could feel the weight of his stare on her and it freaked her the hell out.

Carly lifted her head and her gaze cut to the right. Sure enough, Curtis Thatch was there. His expression seemed concerned. His gaze all dark and intense. And he even took a step toward her.

"Don't!" The word snapped out from her immediately. He froze and several nearby FBI officers tensed.

She should have felt safe. After all, she was in the FBI office. What place was safer? But Curtis was too close, and safe was the last thing she felt.

Curtis held up his hands. "I won't hurt you, I swear."

Was she supposed to buy that line?

She hunched her shoulders and sank deeper into the chair. A chair in Victor's office—well, what he'd said was his temporary office, anyway. And what was Curtis doing being so close? Skulking around?

Just like his brother...

"If you give me five minutes," he said as he crept closer, "I won't press charges against Ethan."

Her heart nearly stopped.

Slowly, her gaze went back to him.

"Five minutes," Curtis said, nodding. "That's all I ask for. Surely Ethan's freedom is worth that small amount of time to you?"

It was.

"But I don't want to talk here," Curtis continued, glancing over his shoulder at the nearby FBI agents. "Everyone and their mother could be listening. Neither of us wants that."

She wasn't sure what she wanted. No, she knew. *Ethan's freedom.*

"I'll tell the agents—right now—that I'm not pressing charges. That it was all a mistake. Then I want you to walk out of this place with me. We'll go to a diner down the road, and you'll give me my five minutes."

He must think she was insane. "I'm supposed to just walk away with you?"

His lips tightened. "I am not Quincy."

No, if he was...he'd have a knife in his chest.

"We'll stay in public the whole time," Curtis promised. "I won't even touch you. I just want to talk. Your lover's freedom for a five minute conversation. That is more than fair."

Her gaze slid around the small room. Victor had been in there before, right before he'd rushed off to interrogate Ethan. Only before he'd left for that interrogation, Victor had secured his weapon in the top desk drawer. She'd watched him lock that weapon up.

And then head in to interrogate Ethan, determination apparent in every hard line of his body.

Ethan can't be locked up.

"Five minutes," she agreed. "Go tell the agents, *right now,* that you aren't pressing charges."

He sucked in a sharp breath, then he whirled and hurried away. Carly leapt to her feet and headed for the drawer. Ethan had taught her so many useful skills when she'd been younger. It took her ten seconds and one bent paperclip to open that drawer...

And then she was rushing out of that office. She came up behind Curtis just as she heard him tell an FBI agent, "No, no there was a mistake at the scene. The man was obviously confused because of the explosion. I don't believe he ever intended to attack me. I won't be pressing charges..."

The young FBI agent stared at him in shock.

"Agent Monroe knows how to reach me. I-I answered all of his questions before, and if he needs me, he can find me easily at my hotel." Curtis gave a quick nod. "But I have to go. Excuse me..."

The FBI agent called out after him. Curtis didn't stop. He went right down the stairs.

While others scrambled to go find Agent Monroe and let him know about Curtis's sudden one-eighty, Carly slipped away, too.

The weight of the gun at the base of her back was incredibly reassuring.

How long would it be before Victor realized she'd swiped it?

***

Sonofabitch. Victor Monroe knew he was between a rock—and a fucking deranged asshole named Ethan Barclay. He stomped out of the interrogation room. Ethan Barclay had been on the FBI's radar for years—a slick piece of work who never left enough evidence behind to actually get charged with anything, though there were sure plenty of suspicions surrounding the guy.

And now, well, the FBI had him for two cases of assault. He'd attacked Curtis Thatch in front of a crowd. Though, to be honest, Victor didn't exactly trust Thatch, not for a second.

But Ethan had made a double screw-up by coming at an FBI agent. There was no way the guy would be walking after that stunt. Victor's superiors at the FBI were about to piss themselves, they were so happy. Only...

Zoe.

Her image flashed before his eyes. Zoe—with her long, dark hair, her green eyes, her sensual features...He'd made a deal with Zoe, and, even more importantly, with Zoe's father, criminal kingpin Luther Bates. Luther would keep cooperating with the FBI under one condition— Zoe had to stay alive.

Fuck. Okay, so he *could* drop the charges against Ethan Barclay. No assaulting an officer charge. His superiors would freak, but they could still keep Ethan on the attack against Curtis Thatch. They could—

"Agent Monroe?"

He spun around. One of the younger FBI agents stared nervously at him.

"Problem, sir," he said.

"I am not in the mood for any more problems."

The guy swallowed. "Dr. Thatch just said he wasn't pressing charges. That it was all some big mistake. He told me Barclay got confused after the bombing, and Thatch said he didn't think the man meant to hurt him."

Hell, yes, Barclay had meant to hurt him. If the FBI hadn't arrived. Barclay would have pulverized the guy.

Victor tried to breathe deeply. Very deeply. "I want to talk with Carly Shay."

"Yes, sir." The red-haired agent almost saluted before he ran away. Victor rolled his eyes. New recruits were so freaking eager.

Carly could help to shed light on Ethan and just what the guy might do if he got out of that interrogation room. Victor suspected that Carly had been raped by Quincy Atkins. Her attack would sure explain Barclay's rage toward the man—and toward Curtis. From the way Ethan watched Carly, Victor understood that the guy was in deep with Carly. Did he love her? Hell, Victor wasn't even sure Ethan could love. But there was some kind of connection there. Maybe it was lust. Maybe it was obsession. Maybe it was some other twisted shit that he didn't understand, but one thing was certain—Carly was Ethan's link to sanity. Victor got that and if she could help them—

The agent ran back. His face was flushed. "She's gone, sir."

"No." An immediate denial.

"She-she must have slipped out when we were dealing with Dr. Thatch."

Victor rushed into his office. He'd left her in there so she would feel *safe*. He'd wanted to reassure her. But there was nothing reassuring about that empty office. He stalked around his desk. "Dammit!" Barclay wouldn't cooperate at all when he learned she was gone. And with Curtis Thatch not pressing charges...

I am screwed.

Then he glanced down and saw that his top desk drawer was open, just a bit. His thundering heartbeat filled his ears as he slowly curled his fingers around that drawer and opened it fully.

His weapon was missing.

My weapon's gone. Carly Shay is gone, and she knew where my weapon was stored. Fuck. And Curtis Thatch just walked out the door. Maybe Carly wasn't the one keeping Ethan sane.

Maybe he was the one watching out for her. "Release Ethan Barclay," he ordered. "Right the hell now."

CHAPTER SEVEN

Ethan sauntered out of the interrogation room. Victor stood just a few feet away, glowering. "So glad to hear that this misunderstanding was cleared up," Ethan said smoothly. "And I—"

"Curtis Thatch dropped the charges against you." Victor's eyes glinted as he delivered his news. "He left about twenty minutes ago, right around the same time that Carly Shay disappeared from the building."

Oh, hell, no. Ethan steeled his expression. "If you'll excuse me, I have pressing business to attend to..." He didn't wait for a response but hurried toward the elevator. Carly was gone? And Thatch had just dropped the charges?

The elevator doors began to close on him, but, before they could seal completely, Victor surged inside the elevator.

Then the doors closed.

"I didn't get to talk with Thatch. He dropped the charges while I was inside with your sorry ass," Victor fired at him.

That means someone else got him to make a deal—Carly? What had she done to get Curtis to drop the charges? And where had she gone?

"Something else you should know," Victor said. "I think Carly took my gun with her when she left."

Fuck.

"Security checks when you come in this building and when you go out, but I'm guessing Carly is a woman with hidden talents, right? Getting a gun past security probably wouldn't be too hard for her."

No, it probably wouldn't be. When she'd been a teen, he'd taught her far too many illegal tricks. Tricks that she would no doubt remember now.

The elevator dinged when it reached the floor. The doors slid open. Ethan advanced, but then Victor threw up an arm, stopping him. "Just so we're clear," Victor rasped. "If anything at all happens to Zoe Peters, I will destroy you."

Ethan turned his head and met Victor's stare. "I'm trying to help her." He liked Zoe. She'd been dealt a terrible hand in life, a fate he understood all too well. They'd both grown up hard, and when he'd met Zoe, he'd recognized a fellow survivor. He'd learned later that Zoe had been running from her past. From the shadow of her deadly father.

Some shadows always followed you. No matter what you did to shake them.

"Now get the hell out of my way," Ethan ordered. Because he had to find Carly. She was his priority.

And if she was out there, armed with a gun...
Curtis Thatch needed to be very afraid.

***

The diner was deserted. The lunch crowd had already come in and gone, so when Carly walked inside, it was easy to spot Curtis Thatch in the back booth.

He waved her over. Waved, as if they were having a perfectly normal meeting. She was still covered in ash and she smelled like fire. Carly was pretty sure she had plenty of scrapes lining her body and the guy was cheerily waving to her.

And she went to him. She slid into the booth and a waitress appeared. The woman didn't give Carly's bedraggled appearance even a second glance. She took Carly's coffee order and walked away.

I don't have money to pay her. That thought froze Carly as she sat there and shame burned through her.

"It's okay," Curtis said, giving her a wan smile as if he'd just read her mind. "I've got this."

She stared across that table at him. He was a lot smaller than his brother. An athletic build, not the hulking shape that Quincy had been. The eyes were the same, but the face was different, too. Softer. Handsome, in one of those non-threatening, easy ways.

Goosebumps rose onto her arms as she stared at him.

"I used to hate you," Curtis said. Then he shook his head. "Wait, that's not right. When I realized my brother had to be dead, I hated the person who had killed him."

You're looking at her.

His gaze swept over her face. "What did my brother do to you?"

She didn't want to tell the story again. The wound just kept opening. But this man...maybe he should hear about the truth. "Quincy Atkins was a sadistic freak. I danced at his club. I was seventeen. *Seventeen.* I was desperate and I needed money to survive."

She should have gone to Ethan. He would have helped her, but back then, he'd been struggling too. When Ethan found out what she'd been doing, he'd put a stop to it.

But it had been too late.

"Quincy got obsessed."

Curtis glanced down at the table. "He...he did that. Found women that he wanted. Couldn't let go."

Women... "I was seventeen," she whispered again. She couldn't take her gaze off him right then.

Curtis slowly looked back up at her. "He attacked you."

"I was going home. A car pulled up behind me—a van." *Just like that freaking van in the parking garage.* "Men grabbed me. They tied me up. They took me to him." She swallowed, battling those memories. "When he got obsessed with the others, did he do that to them, too?"

Curtis had paled. "I'm afraid now, that he did." His voice had gone hoarse. "I've found out...other women were missing back then."

Her chest iced. She'd always wondered...no, she'd always known, if she and Ethan hadn't gotten away, they would have been dead.

"He's dead," Curtis said slowly.

She could feel the weight of the gun at her back, but it was just that, a weight. She didn't need to grab it. Curtis wasn't threatening her. He was just before her, looking sad, his shoulders hunched.

"I'm sorry," Curtis told her.

At first, Carly thought she had to be mistaken. She shook her head.

But then he said it again. "I'm sorry." Now his voice was stronger. "For what you've gone through. For all that's happened to you. One of Quincy's old gang, he contacted me about a week ago. Told me that news was leaking, saying you and Ethan Barclay had been the ones to kill Q."

We were.

"I needed to see you for myself. I even..." His jaw clenched. "I followed you around town. Like a freaking stalker. But it won't be happening again. Q is gone, and we're done with the past. *I'm* done with it. You won't get trouble from me, and I'm going to spread word that the past is dead. I don't want anyone else coming after you, either."

Her cheeks flamed red-hot, then seemed to go ice cold. She'd feared this man, but he'd just wanted closure. She couldn't even blame him for that. "The bomb," Carly whispered. "Who set it?"

He shook his head. "I don't know. Maybe it wasn't even meant for you. Maybe it was just for Ethan." His lips hitched into a tired half-smile. "The man has plenty of enemies."

No, that wasn't making sense to her. "Dr. Nelson called me. He said the bomb was there, that I had to get out." That meant the bomb had been set to kill her, right?

"I don't know any Dr. Nelson," Curtis said, sounding confused.

The waitress appeared. She put coffee down in front of them both. Carly reached out quickly, her hands curling around the mug and absorbing some desperately needed warmth.

She was being hunted. So was Ethan. Only he'd suspected the main threat was Curtis, and that didn't seem to be the case.

Curtis leaned toward her. His hand lifted and curled around hers as she clasped the coffee mug. She couldn't help but tense at his touch. "I want to help you," Curtis said. "Maybe we should go—"

"Maybe you should take your hand off her." The order was delivered in a deceptively soft voice. One laced with a quiet and unmistakable fury.

Carly turned her head. Ethan was there. She hadn't even seen him approach the table, much less enter the diner. She wondered how he'd found her—she didn't even have a phone on her for him to track. The phone had been smashed to hell and back at Reflections.

Then she got a good look at his face. His expression was cut in hard lines of rage, and his eyes gleamed as he glared at Curtis.

Carly didn't wait for Curtis to pull his hand away. She jumped to her feet. "It's not what you think!" She moved to stand in front of Ethan, forcing him to look at her. "He doesn't want to hurt me. He isn't...he isn't like Quincy."

But Ethan shook his head. "You don't know that. You just met the guy."

Okay, excellent point. She glanced over her shoulder at Curtis. He hadn't moved, but he had paled. A glare from Ethan could make plenty of people pale.

"I don't want trouble with you," Curtis said, gazing up at Ethan. "Not with you or her. I-I made peace with my past now, and I'm ready to move on."

It seemed to Carly that everyone in the diner—the few stragglers there, anyway—they were all quiet and watching the exchange, as if they'd sensed danger when Ethan had first spoken.

"Then get moving," Ethan ordered him. "Because I don't want to see you around her again."

Her shoulders tensed. She didn't like that wording. Didn't like the possessive, ownership tone that Ethan had. Yes, they were in a serious situation, but Ethan needed to start backing the hell off that territorial thing.

Curtis rose—slowly. Then his head inclined toward her. "You won't have any trouble from me."

A door to her past was finally closing and the relief she felt was pretty heavy.

Curtis walked away.

Silence lingered in his wake.

"Carly..." Ethan gritted out. "Do you have any idea how much you just scared me? It's a good thing Charles was tailing you."

Charles. So *that* was how he'd found her. Ethan had made sure that her movements were monitored, even when he'd been in federal custody. She turned to fully face him. Carly tilted her head back to better look up at him. "I get that you worry about me."

"Worry doesn't even come close—"

"I worry about you, too. Worry so much that I promised Curtis a sit-down if he'd just drop the charges against you."

Shock flashed across Ethan's face.

"You're welcome," she muttered. Then she glanced down at the table. Curtis had tossed some cash near the mugs of coffee. Great. She could slink out of that place and go crash. Because after her night and her morning—she desperately needed to crash.

She strode for the door. When she stepped outside, she wasn't particularly surprised to see Agent Monroe standing there. Seemed right.

He lifted his brows and held out his hand.

Crap.

Her step quickened as she headed toward him. "Are you going to lock me up for this?"

"So far, only you, Ethan, and I know what you did..."

She put the gun in his hand. He inclined his head. Then he glanced over her shoulder, at Ethan. Carly had been aware of Ethan following close behind her. "Put this in the 'I Owe Victor' column," the agent ordered. "And make damn sure you're paying that debt."

Ethan always paid his debts. She knew that.

Ethan's hand slid to the small of her back. He urged her toward the car parked near the curb— the gleaming car and Charles. Well, at least the gang was all back together. And what a twisted, battered gang it was. She took a step, then stopped. Her gaze slid back to Victor. "Do you have any idea where Keith Nelson is right now?"

Victor shook his head.

"He called me." Her smashed phone had been collected by the FBI at Reflections. *What was left of Reflections.* "He knew I was inside Reflections so he had to be close by, watching me."

"I think so..."

"He knows who set the bomb."

"Finding him is a top goal for me, I assure you."

Ethan's hand moved to curl around her waist. "Stopping the bomber is a top goal for *me,*" Ethan said.

Ethan and Carly climbed into the car. Through the window, she saw Victor watching them as they pulled away.

The car cut through the city, and the silence
in that vehicle was far too thick and heavy.
Finally, when that silence was about to shatter
her nerves, she glanced at Ethan.

His gaze was on her. She knew it had been, all
along.

"I don't want you taking any risks for me,"
Ethan said.

Carly rubbed her sweaty palms against her
legs. "And I don't want you controlling me."

Surprise flickered in his eyes.

She laughed. "Do you even realize you do it?
Or are you so used to giving orders that you think
it's normal? It's not. I get that we've got a
dangerous enemy out there. I get that things are
screwed up and scary, but..." This needed to be
said. "You don't control me, Ethan. If I want to
help you, I will. If I want to face my own demons,
I will. You won't stop me."

His gaze slid away from her. "I don't want to
control you."

Liar, liar.

"I just want you safe. When I realized you
were gone with Curtis, I was afraid you'd be
dead—no, I was afraid you'd kill *him,* and then I
wouldn't be able to help you."

She inched closer to him. Finally, she felt as if
all of the walls had been pushed down between
them. "Why, Ethan?" Time for brutal honesty.
"Were you worried you wouldn't be able to make
that body disappear for me this time?"

He flinched.

Carly reached out and threaded her fingers with his. "I should have gone to the police years ago. Right after Quincy died. I should have told them everything. I was defending myself. I wouldn't have gone to jail." *But hiding the body, covering up the act*...those were crimes that she could be sentenced for committing.

Ethan shook his head. "I didn't make the body disappear because of the cops. I can handle them. I did it because I knew that if Quincy's allies found out what we'd done, they'd come after you. Having his body vanish gave them doubt. It protected you. That's all I've ever wanted to do," he said, voice deepening. "*Just protect you.*"

But he couldn't protect her from everything, just as she couldn't protect him.

It wasn't just about them, though. Not anymore. "We need to find Nelson." He was the key they needed.

Ethan's fingers squeezed hers, and he nodded.

***

Charles took them back to Carly's place. He opened the door for her, and his face had its usual stoic expression. During their talk in the back seat, Ethan had kept the security screen in place, but she suspected that Charles was aware of her secrets. He was Ethan's trusted guard—how could he not know?

"So you had my back," Carly asked Charles, "when I went off with Curtis?" She'd never even seen him tailing her.

Charles inclined his head. His eyes were a warm brown, and they seemed to soften as he stared at her.

"Thank you," Carly told him.

"Just doing my job."

Ethan had come around the car and was heading her way.

"Is your job protecting me?" Carly asked Charles. "I thought it was protecting Ethan."

"Things aren't always what they seem," Charles murmured.

A shiver slid down her spine. Then Ethan took her arm and they headed inside her building. She and Ethan didn't speak again, not until they were right in front of her door. Then she stopped him and asked, "Is it safe for me to trust Charles?"

Ethan laughed. "Is this question because my last bodyguard turned out to be a psycho killer who gave me all my lovely scars?"

She just stared at him.

He smiled. "There's this really good detective in D.C. Her name is Faith Chestang. She's the one who recommended Charles to me. He's her cousin."

He'd hired a cop's cousin? Didn't he think that was a bit...risky?

At her expression, Ethan laughed again. "Oh, baby, of *course*, I know he's an undercover FBI agent. Seriously, how could I not?"

Her jaw dropped.

"But who better to watch my ass? And yours? Especially with trouble closing in around you. Besides..." He rolled back his shoulders. "I think Charles is softening toward me. He'd better watch it, or the guy may even start to like me."

"He's FBI..." And they'd just talked about disposing of a body while the guy had been driving the car. To think, Ethan had once been worried about listening devices at her place. Now he didn't seem to care at all what the FBI learned. *What is happening here?*

"Don't worry," Ethan assured her. "I've got this covered."

She doubted it.

Ethan's hand lifted and his knuckles skimmed over her jaw. "You know, we could walk away right now. Me and you. I could make us both vanish. We could go to some tropical island. Get naked. And let the rest of the world fall away."

He wasn't serious. Wait, was he? Because that offer sounded pretty good to her. With her body aching and fear still surrounding her like a cloak, the idea of going someplace else, of just slipping away, it sure sounded like a prime option. Too tempting.

Ethan bent toward her. "We can do it," he said. "Just say the word."

Instead of speaking, she pushed up on her toes and her lips pressed to his. It was a quick kiss. Hot and fast. "Thank you for saving me at Reflections."

He blinked. His golden eyes seemed to smolder.

"I didn't miss that whole protecting-me-with-your-body routine," she said softly and then she kissed him again. "But how about you don't do that again? Because I rather like it when you're alive and safe, too."

He licked her lower lip. "Can't make a promise like that. I'd take any damn wound, for you."

That scared her. Parts of Ethan—he could scare her straight to her soul. "And don't attack again," she said.

He stilled.

"The way you went after Curtis...it was like something had switched off inside of you." For an instant, he'd lost control. She knew it. An uncontrolled Ethan was a dangerous thing.

"I thought he'd tried to kill you." His voice roughened as he added, "And when I stared in his eyes, for just a minute, I was back in that shitty room, looking up at Quincy and waiting for the SOB to kill me. It all came back to me. The hate, the fear, the rage. Something...shit, you're right, something snapped in me." His forehead pressed to hers. "Because I could never stand it if someone hurt you that way again. It fucking gutted us both before."

Yes, it had.

But they were different now. Stronger. They'd survived the fire. Survived hell. They could do it again.

"I don't trust Curtis," Ethan said. "Not for an instant, and I'm hoping like hell that Charles and his FBI buddies are tearing apart Curtis's life right now. Because I'm not the only one with skeletons hiding in my closet."

No, she didn't think that he was. She knew now—thanks to bitter, painful experience—that everyone carried around skeletons. Some folks were just better at hiding them.

Worry still pushed at her. "Is it even safe to have this conversation out here?" He'd been so worried about bugs before—

"I'm handling the FBI."

She really wanted to know more. But that more could happen inside her place, not in the hallway. Her closest neighbor was gone, but other folks were still nearby. She pushed open the door to her place. She flipped on the lights and—

"*Help...me...*"

Blood was on her floor. Blood and Keith Nelson's wounded body. He was slumped near her sofa.

"*Help...*" He gasped once more.

Ethan and Carly ran toward him. But as soon as Keith saw Ethan, he let out a long, horror-filled scream. "*No!* Stay a-away!"

Ethan just kept going forward. Keith swung at him, fighting hard, but Ethan grabbed his arms and held tightly. "Calm the hell down! I want to help you!" He glanced over at Carly. "Go get Charles. He'll have backup here faster than either of us will."

Because help always came faster for the FBI?

She whirled for the door.

"No!" Keith yelled. "Don't leave me...*with him!*"

His voice was so desperate that Carly glanced back over her shoulder. Keith appeared utterly terrified. He was thrashing around, twisting and jerking. He was already bleeding so much—Keith had to calm down or his injuries would just be far worse.

"If you leave me..." Keith cried. "He'll...finish...*Kill me...*"

"No," Carly said. "You're wrong!" Ethan hadn't been the one to attack Keith.

But Keith was frantic, so wild. Twisting and screaming and mumbling about Ethan killing him.

She stared at him, lost, but in the next moment, Keith collapsed. His eyes sagged closed, and he fell back against the carpet. No more accusations. No more fear.

"Is he dead?" Carly asked. He barely seemed to be breathing.

"Not yet," Ethan growled. "Go! Get him help!"

She ran as fast as she could. In moments, she was flying out of her building, and, sure enough, Charles was there, waiting near the curb. When he saw her, he immediately leapt forward. "Call for backup!" she yelled at him.

She saw his eyelids flicker. "Back-up?" Charles asked carefully, then shook his head. "You want more of Ethan's men—"

"I want an ambulance! And if you want the FBI here, get them, too! Keith Nelson is bleeding out on my living room floor!"

He yanked out his phone.

She didn't stop to see who he called. She rushed back inside. Keith needed help. The guy had to survive. He'd seen the man who was after her and Ethan. He knew the bomber's identity.

And despite what Keith had said...the bad guy wasn't Ethan!

The real attacker was out there. They just had to find him.

She raced back to her room. Her door was still ajar. But when she got inside...

Keith was on the floor. Blood was all around him.

But Ethan—Ethan was gone.

CHAPTER EIGHT

"According to Keith Nelson..." Victor said, his voice mild, "he doesn't remember who attacked him. He doesn't remember calling you and warning you about the bomb. Hell, the last thing the guy can clearly remember is Ethan Barclay, telling him that if he saw Keith again, then the doc would be getting an ass kicking."

Carly glanced toward Keith's hospital room. She'd ridden over with him in the ambulance, and when the doctors had taken him back, she'd waited with Charles.

Charles...who was no longer pretending to be hired muscle for Ethan.

"Is that why he freaked out when he saw Ethan?" Carly asked. "Because he woke up and thought Ethan had kicked his ass?"

Victor shrugged. "Can't say for sure. It would certainly help matters out if Ethan were here to answer that question for me."

The suspicion in his voice just made her even angrier. "There's no way Ethan attacked Keith! Ethan and I were together nearly the whole time and—"

"Why did he vanish, Carly?" Charles asked her softly.

Victor slanted a quick glance his way.

"Why did he abandon you?" Charles pressed. "I thought he actually cared about you. I bought into that act."

Maybe Ethan was right. Maybe Charles had been softening toward him.

"Then he threw you to the wolves."

Her spine stiffened. "He knew the FBI was about to swarm. The victim was yelling that *Ethan* was to blame. Maybe he just didn't want to get tossed back into interrogation again."

Charles nodded. "Right. So he abandoned you."

"No! He didn't!" She didn't know what the hell had happened. Going back to her home, seeing that Ethan was gone...it made no sense to her.

"He's looking after himself," Victor surmised. "This is the point where you have to do the same thing. You have to watch your own ass." He put his hand on her shoulder. "Are you ready to talk to me? To really tell me all you know about Quincy Atkins and Ethan Barclay?"

Hell, no, she wasn't. Her temples were pounding, and she was *worried* about Ethan. "How did Keith get in my apartment?" She wanted to shrug off his hand, but forced herself to stay still. *He thinks he's helping me.* He was wrong, though. The one who could help her?

Ethan.

But he's vanished.

No, it just wasn't right. Ethan wouldn't leave her.

Victor and Charles exchanged a long look.

"The guy doesn't remember," Victor said.

"The door was locked." She remembered unlocking it. "He was at least ten feet from that door."

"Uh, about Ethan..."

"I didn't search the apartment," she whispered as fear grew within her. "I didn't even stop to think that Keith's attacker could still be there! What if he was waiting for me to leave? What if he did something to Ethan?"

Charles looked doubtful. "It's not easy to get the drop on Ethan Barclay."

"And what would the attacker even do with his body?" Victor's hand fell from her shoulder. "Sorry, look, I get that you're trying to explain away his abandonment, but the guy vanished on his own free will. He wasn't dragged off. He's six foot two and close to two hundred pounds. It wouldn't be easy to drag him any place."

Her heart was racing fast. Too fast. Fear had a choking grasp on her. "It depends on where you're dragging him." Then she turned away from the FBI agents. She started walking down the hospital corridor. Then she started running.

They called after her. She didn't stop.

Something had happened to Ethan. He hadn't abandoned her. She wouldn't believe that.

She'd always trusted him. She wouldn't lose faith in him now.

***

He was tied up. Bound to a chair. The ropes cut into his arms and legs. Ethan slowly opened his eyes. His head hurt like a bitch, throbbing constantly—because some SOB had hit him over the head. He'd been trying to help that freaking shrink, and he'd heard the creak of the floor too late.

By the time Ethan had tried to turn, it had been too late.

Now he was in darkness. Total freaking darkness. But he could feel the ropes and as he flexed his hands, testing those bounds, Ethan also heard...

Someone else breathing.

"Did you think I'd let you walk away?" That voice was low. Taunting.

The lights flashed on. Too bright, blinding Ethan for an instant. He blinked frantically, and then he found himself staring at a familiar face.

A face he'd pounded before.

And Carly said I shouldn't have attacked the SOB.

He yanked on the ropes.

"I know how it ended, you see. I knew all along, but I wanted a confession. I was sent a video—a video of you and Carly Shay killing my brother."

Fuck. He'd thought he destroyed that evidence.

"What? No cry of surprise? Did you *know* that you'd been caught on the security feed at that warehouse so long ago?"

He'd known. Too late.

"Carly was the one tied in the chair, wasn't she? You were on the floor. Bleeding. Dying. Carly screamed and begged. She promised Quincy *anything* if he would let you live..."

He jerked in the chair. It rocked forward, then backward on its legs.

"And then I learned that she was still hung up on you. After all these years, still *involved* with you. That's when I knew the way to hurt her. Really gut her. "

Fucking bastard.

"When you two ran out of Reflections together, after I saw—first-hand—just what it was like between you, I knew exactly how to punish dear Carly."

"Your bomb didn't fucking work! We got out!"

Curtis laughed. "I wanted you out. The bomb was meant to scare. To be a distraction, nothing more. The fact that your business burned to the ground? That was pure bonus." His laughter faded. "But I saw the way you two were together, and I knew just what I had to do."

"What you had to do?" Ethan muttered. "Was it *talk* me to death?'

"The way to really break her..." Curtis smiled at Ethan. "The way to break her...is by breaking you."

Ethan just stared back at the bastard. "I'm not easy to break. Kind of a been there, done that with me. But, hey, you're obviously feeling all bat-shit crazy, so give it your best shot."

The guy's smile dimmed.

Ethan glanced around as he tried to assess his escape option. There wasn't a whole lot of furniture in the room. Just the chair he was tied to and some kind of instrument tray to the side. He could see the gleam of metal over there. A scalpel. And some other rather twisted looking utensils.

Plastic had been taped down on the floor around him. And more plastic covered the walls. Ethan whistled. "Did your big brother teach you how to set up a kill scene like this one?" The better to avoid the problem of blood spatter once the victims started that pesky bleeding and dying.

"I taught *him,*" Curtis barked. "Quincy was an idiot. I was—"

"The brains." Like he hadn't heard others claim similar over the years. "Whatever, I don't—"

Curtis yanked a scalpel from that exam tray. He leaned close to Ethan. "I made those girls vanish."

Ethan frowned at him. "Girls?"

"Quincy fucked them, but then he gave them to me. I got to cut them open. I got to see all of them."

He was seeing a seriously deranged fuck. "And you made it as a doctor?" *A trauma surgeon.* A guy who sliced for his living had also cut for his pleasure.

"Why do you think I became a doctor?" Curtis had that sick grin back in place. "I do enjoy my work."

Ethan was still tugging at the ropes. He'd get out, sooner or later. He was just hoping for sooner. Before Curtis fucked him up too much. He already had enough scars without adding more to his body.

"But everything changed when Quincy vanished. I always suspected you were involved. And now, it's judgment day. You die, you pay. And poor little Carly will get the news that you've vanished completely." Curtis laughed again, the sound high and bitter. "Do you think she'll believe you just deserted her? Probably, at first. But later, when I'm ready for her to really suffer...maybe I'll send her a few pieces of you that I keep."

"And people think I'm the psycho," Ethan said, whistling.

"He was my brother!"

"Like I give a shit. He was a twisted, murdering prick, and he got exactly what he deserved." Ethan wasn't about to show fear. He didn't feel any. He did feel pissed. "And you're going to get what you deserve, too." His voice was low, lethal. Promising. "Unless you kill me outright, I'll get free. I'll take that scalpel that you're holding in your hand, and I'll use it to cut your throat. You'll be bleeding and choking and I'll just watch you die."

Curtis had frozen. "You think you can manipulate me," he finally murmured. "You're *trying* to make me kill you quickly so that you won't suffer, but it won't work that way. You will suffer. You will beg. And there will be no mercy."

Ethan couldn't shrug because of the way he was tied to the chair. "Keep thinking that, if you want. The truth is, I just told you what's going to happen in this room."

Curtis hesitated. For an instant, fear flashed on his face. The guy was used to giving out pain, but he didn't seem to like the idea of being on the receiving end of that scalpel.

"The bomb you set," Ethan said. "It could have killed Carly." The guy said he'd meant for them to get out—Ethan didn't know if he believed that bull. He thought Curtis would've been plenty happy if they'd been blown to hell. "Here's the thing..." Ethan lowered his voice.

Curtis stepped forward.

That's right, bastard, come closer.

"You aren't the first SOB to tie me up and try to torture me. *My* own brother did that shit to me."

Fascination. That was what he saw in Curtis's eyes. The man crept forward a little more. The scalpel lowered in his hand.

"I heard a story about that..." Curtis's gaze darted to the scars on Ethan's cheeks. "But he didn't cut you deep enough."

"Not on my face, he didn't," Ethan agreed. "But I've got more scars. Deep wounds."

Curtis came forward more. So close now...

Too close...

"Show me," Curtis said. His eyes were eager.

I'll fucking show you plenty.

Ethan slammed his head into Curtis's face and heard the crunch of cartilage as the man's nose broke. Curtis screamed and fell back as blood gushed down his face.

***

"The crime scene team is still here!" Charles said as he followed right behind Carly. They were back at the brownstone, and, yes, the guy was right. Crime techs were in her place. So was a nice, big yellow line of police tape, barring her door. "Ethan is not in there!" Charles told her.

No, not in my home but—

She stopped in the hallway. "Did you hear that?" Slowly, she turned away from her door. In that one instant, she'd heard...

Charles eyed her as if she were mentally unstable.

"I heard someone scream," Carly said definitely. She was sure of it. Carly pointed to the door right across the hall from her place. "My neighbor Katherine is in Europe for the next month. Ethan owns this building, so that means he owns her space."

"Uh, yeah, what does that have to do with—"

"No one should be in there right now." She rushed to that apartment and twisted the doorknob. It was locked so she started pounding on the door.

Charles grabbed her arm and pulled her back. "What are you doing?"

"I heard a scream come from that apartment." Now there was only silence.

Charles shook his head. "No, you didn't, you—"

"Carly!"

That voice—that roar. It was *Ethan's* voice. And Charles had just stiffened. He'd heard the sound, too. The roar had come from inside the apartment that should have been empty. She grabbed for the door knob again. Twisted it frantically and started pounding on the locked door. "Ethan, Ethan! I'm here! I'm coming to help you!" Behind her, she could hear Charles talking on his phone, asking for help at the scene. *"Ethan!"* She started kicking that damn door. She was getting in to him—one way or another.

***

The ropes were still too tight on him. That shit needed to give way soon because Curtis was back on his feet. Blood poured from his nose and the guy swiped it away.

"Look what the fuck you did!" Curtis raged.

Ethan smiled at him. "Going to do a whole lot more. I told you, I'm going to be the one standing soon and just watching you die."

"Ethan!"

He stiffened at that cry. Carly. He'd heard her outside and he'd yelled for her, an instinctive thing. But now he wished that he'd kept quiet because a sinister smile had curled Curtis's lips.

"Full circle," Curtis whispered. He bent and picked up the scalpel he'd dropped. His blood spattered down on the plastic-covered floor.

Carly was pounding on the door. It sounded like she was trying to rip that door open. That was his Carly. So fierce and determined.

"Maybe it's meant to be this way," Curtis murmured, giving his head a rough shake. "It should end the same way, don't you think?" Curtis asked him. The false veil of his sanity was gone, and Ethan knew he was seeing the real monster that the man had always been.

"I think you're nuts!"

"Only Carly isn't tied in the chair. You are."

He wanted that rope *gone*.

"So when she gets in...and don't worry, I'll make sure she comes in...she'll see you. Then *she'll* be the one on the floor. She'll be the one I torture and kick. My brother kicked you, didn't he? I saw it on the video. He kicked you in your ribs and sweet Carly promised to do *anything* if he stopped hurting you." More blood poured from his nose. "Will you promise *anything* for her?"

Carly can't be alone out there. She has to have help. The FBI wouldn't just let her rush out alone, not with all the shit that was happening. Would they?

Then Curtis turned away from him, and Ethan saw the gun that was tucked in the back of the man's pants. "*Get away!*" Ethan bellowed, hoping she could hear him. "*Carly, get away!*" She couldn't come in there.

Curtis carefully put the scalpel down on the instrument tray. And he took out his gun. "Let's see if you'll do anything..."

"No," Ethan whispered. "Don't."

"Ready to beg?"

Ethan yanked at his ropes. He could feel blood on his wrists. He just yanked harder and the rope cut deeper into him. Harder...

He heard the front door burst in. "Carly, no, get back!" Ethan yelled. *Please, baby, back.* "He's got a—"

Carly wasn't the one who rushed into the room first. Charles was. And Charles was armed, too. But Charles had his gaze locked on Ethan and he didn't even see Curtis because that tricky sonofabitch had moved into the corner of the room, *behind* Charles as the guy rushed to Ethan's side.

"No, Charles! Gun, *gun—*"

The gun exploded. A bullet slammed into Charles, hitting him in the back. Ethan was staring right at the FBI agent when the bullet struck him. He saw the flare of Charles's eyes. The shock and the pain that covered his face. Charles tried to whirl in order to confront his attacker, but Curtis was just laughing and stepping forward as he fired again.

A bullet sank into Charles's shoulder.

The gun fell from the agent's hand.

Curtis advanced one step more, his gun still aimed at Charles. "Not the way I usually like to kill, but—"

He didn't get a chance to fire another shot at Charles because Carly had just slammed into his body. She hit him hard and they tumbled to the floor. This time, Curtis was the one to lose the gun and Carly attacked him with a wild fury. Punching and kicking and scratching.

"Charles, get the fuck up!" Ethan said, fear filling him—fear for Carly and Charles. Because Charles wasn't moving now. He'd slumped on the floor, and Ethan was afraid that bullet to the back had hit the agent's spine. *No, no.* "Charles!"

And then he heard the laughter. That damn mocking laughter from Curtis.

Curtis was bigger and stronger than Carly, and he had her pinned beneath him on the floor. "You should have never killed my brother," Curtis said, panting as he fought to hold her. Carly was still fighting, hell, yes, she was. Ethan knew she would always keep fighting.

"Your brother is burning...in hell," Carly threw back at him.

Curtis pulled back his fist, and it looked as if the bastard was about to slam that fist right into Carly's face. That would be only the first of what he had planned for Carly.

"*Don't!*" Ethan yelled.

Curtis smiled. "Got to promise me...*anything.* Got to beg. Like she did for you..."

The ropes gave way. Ethan leapt out of that chair. He grabbed the scalpel off the freaking weird-ass surgical tray and he said, "Carly, baby, close your eyes. *Please...*" Because if she didn't, she'd see Ethan for who he truly was.

In the next second, he'd grabbed Curtis's shoulder. He yanked the guy around, and Ethan sliced that scalpel across the man's throat. He pushed as hard as he could when he made that slice, wanting that scalpel to cut deep. *Carving into him.*

A promise is a promise.

Blood sprayed at him and Curtis fell back, grabbing for his throat.

Ethan looked down at Carly. Her eyes were wide open, staring with horror and fear and disgust.

At me.

Curtis was making a choking sound, still struggling, still bleeding, and Ethan glared down at him. "I killed your damn brother. *I'm* the one who shoved the knife all the way in his heart, and I'm also the one who just killed *you.*"

Then the cavalry arrived. More agents came rushing into the apartment. Victor was the first one leading the charge. "Hands up!" Victor yelled. "Up!"

Ethan lifted his hands. The scalpel fell to the floor.

"Sonofabitch," Victor said, voice hushed. "*Sonofabitch.*" Then he shook his head. "Secure him!"

Ethan didn't know if the agent wanted the gasping man on the ground secured—*or me.*

But Victor wasn't even looking at him any longer. He'd rushed over to Charles. "Agent down!" Victor snarled into his phone. "I need an ambulance here, now. *Now!*"

Charles lifted his hand toward Victor. Victor caught his hand and held on tight. "You're going to be all right. It's okay."

Two agents were on the floor, kneeling near Curtis. Another had helped Carly to her feet. Blood was on her shirt. Probably because she'd been so close when Ethan had attacked Curtis.

And a final FBI agent—well, he had his gun on Ethan.

"Will Charles make it?" Ethan asked quietly.

Victor swore. "*He's fine.*"

So Victor was more of a liar than Ethan had thought...and he was also a man who was holding tight to another agent's hand and assuring Charles that everything was going to be all right.

Ethan felt respect stir inside of him. Victor was better than he'd expected.

Carly stood there a moment, seemingly in shock as she looked at Ethan. Horror was still plain to see on her face. This whole scene—it was such a tangled flashback of their past. Only there wouldn't be any chance of hiding the body this time.

No escape.

He'd attacked, and Ethan knew Curtis wouldn't survive much longer. Not even with the agent trying to stop that blood flow.

Carly shook her head, hard, then she turned from Ethan. She hurried and bent near Charles, and she joined Victor in trying to stop *his* blood flow.

Ethan's gaze slid back to Curtis. His eyes narrowed on the man.

After all, he had a promise to keep.

You'll be bleeding and choking and I'll just watch you die.

***

The lights from the ambulances lit up the scene. Two ambulances. Two victims. Both still fighting to live.

Charles was loaded in an ambulance first. Victor insisted on it. Carly could hear him yelling out orders. He even grabbed one of the EMTs and snarled that his agent had better "fucking be his priority".

The EMTs were already working fast and furiously to save Charles. And Charles—he was moving. His legs and his arms moved, and Carly was so grateful that Curtis's bullet hadn't lodged in his spine. When she'd rushed in after Charles and heard the blast of gunfire, she'd been terrified.

And I just grabbed for Curtis. I didn't want him to hurt anyone else.

"He...did it," Charles said, grunting. His gurney was being loaded into the back of the ambulance as Carly watched. She stood outside of her building, blood on her, with too many neighbors and curious bystanders glancing at her with shocked eyes.

She inched closer to the ambulance so that she could better hear Charles.

"Ethan..." Charles said. "Heard...confess...he killed Quincy and he..."

"He used the scalpel on Curtis?" Victor finished. "Yeah, don't worry, buddy, I got that part."

But Charles gave a hard shake of his head. "Saved...*her.*"

She saw Victor's shoulders tense.

"C-Curtis...shot me...would have...killed...all...us..."

She knew that Curtis had wanted her dead. If he'd had his way, yes, Charles was right, Curtis would not have let any of them leave alive.

"Ethan...stopped him..."

Ethan had stopped him, all right. Another sight that Carly would never forget. *He asked me to close my eyes.*

She hadn't. She'd been too afraid to look away. Afraid that in that instant—*I'd lose Ethan.*

"Listen," Victor said, his voice sounding hoarse, "right now, all I want you to do is let the EMTs and the docs do their work, okay? Forget everyone else. Forget the case."

Charles had been loaded securely into the ambulance.

The doors were slammed shut and a few seconds later, the siren screamed on.

Carly jerked at the sound.

"Just concentrate on surviving," Victor said, his voice low, but Carly was so close she caught the words, even though she knew Charles hadn't. He was already gone, rushing away in that ambulance toward the hospital.

She had to blink away the tears in her eyes. She was sick of the death and blood and—

More EMTs burst out of the building. This time, Curtis was on the gurney. Nausea rose within her as she saw him. He wasn't moving, not like Charles had been. In fact, his body was stone still and his skin was ashen.

"I want a guard to stay with him every moment!" Victor bellowed. "That man is dangerous! No risks, *none!* He shot an FBI agent, and he is going to pay!"

Carly thought he was paying. He was dying. Maybe even already dead. He'd be joining his brother soon enough.

A few moments later, the second ambulance left the scene. Victor watched it for a moment, then he whirled to face her. "You knew," he said.

Carly could only shake her head. She wasn't sure what she knew anymore.

But Victor closed that small distance between them. He put his hands on her shoulders. "You knew Ethan wouldn't leave you. And he killed for you...*again,* right? This is the second time?"

She wasn't going to lie or hide, not anymore. She also wasn't going to let Ethan take the blame for her. "I was the one who stabbed Quincy Atkins. Ethan has spent all these years covering *my* crime because he wanted to protect me." Yes, he'd shoved the knife in even deeper, plunging it harder into Quincy's chest, but she knew the truth...*Quincy was already dying then. Ethan just sped up the process.*

She heard the door to the brownstone open behind her. She looked back over her shoulder. Ethan stood there. Ethan—tall, dark, dangerous

Ethan Barclay. His scars glinted under the sunlight. It was the first time she'd looked at him and really seen those scars.

It almost felt as if it were the first time she'd truly seen him at all.

Blood covered his shirt. His hands. Because he'd just sliced open a man's throat with no hesitation.

"Why would he do that?" Victor asked. "Why protect you?"

She swallowed. "Quincy had friends. If they'd known I killed him, they would have come for me. Just like Curtis did..." A deranged psychopath, bent on vengeance.

"Why didn't Ethan throw you to the wolves?"

He was handcuffed. The handcuffs appeared ridiculously fragile around his wrists, and as she stared at his wrists, she could see the blood there. Not blood that had come from Curtis, but Ethan's blood. Because he'd been tied up and he'd fought frantically to get free.

Just as I had, years before.

Curtis had wanted Ethan to beg for her life. But the only time he'd begged, it had been...

When he asked me to close my eyes.

She cleared her throat. "Why didn't he throw me to the wolves?"

One of the agents opened the back door of a police cruiser. Ethan was pushed into the back seat.

"I have a pretty good idea," she murmured.

CHAPTER NINE

He wasn't in interrogation this time. Instead, Ethan was waiting in a small cell, one located in the back of the police station. A federal agent had come to see him hours before, and Ethan had asked to make his phone call.

And with that one call, he'd reached out to his contact in D.C.

Now...now he waited.

The hours had slid past at a snail's pace. He looked down at his hands. The blood was gone now, but he knew exactly what he'd done. He'd killed a man.

And if he had it to do all over, he'd just send the SOB to hell a lot faster. *Before* Curtis had managed to shoot Charles.

There was a window in his cell. A tiny one, lined with bars, near the ceiling. He knew when darkness came because the faint streak of light stopped shining through that window.

He wondered where Carly was. Still with FBI Agent Victor Monroe? Was the FBI agent offering her a new life, maybe some new identity in

Witness Protection? All she'd have to do would be to testify...

Against me.

He hoped she took the deal. He could still see the terrible horror that had been on Carly's face. She would never forget what he'd done. And he couldn't regret the act. After all, Carly was alive now. The threat to her was gone.

Case fucking closed.

He heard the low groan of one of the doors opening down the hallway. Probably a guard, coming to bring him a late dinner.

When he'd made his phone call, he'd been asked if he was calling in his lawyer, Sophie Sarantos, from D.C.

He'd said yes but...

"Ethan Barclay, you sonofabitch..." The feminine voice seemed to echo around him.

A guard hadn't brought him dinner. Instead, his visitor from D.C. had finally arrived, and from the looks of her, she was pissed.

At least she made good time getting here...

Detective Faith Chestang was wearing one of her usual, no-nonsense suits. A truly horrific suit. He'd figured out early, though, that she donned the suits to try and downplay her own attractiveness—like that would ever happen. Her dark hair was pulled back in a bun, and her coffee skin was clear and pretty much ageless—though during his research into Faith's life, he'd discovered that she was actually thirty-five.

And she was also heavily involved with one of the most powerful men in D.C. A man who was at least twenty years her senior.

Another story, though. For another day.

"You're just going to stare at me?" Faith demanded, crossing her arms over her chest. Her badge was clipped to her side. "My cousin was on your detail, and he got shot! Shot! My *favorite* cousin!"

Right. She was definitely pissed. "Sorry?" Ethan offered.

Her eyes turned to slits at that response.

"In my defense," he added, "I did call you right away. I didn't want you to wait on getting official notification and all that crap." He eased toward the bars that separated them. "How is he?"

She huffed out a hard breath. "How do you *think* he is? Charles was shot. Twice. What kind of coward shoots an FBI agent in the back?"

"A dead one."

Her long lashes lowered. "So you already know that Curtis Thatch didn't make it to the hospital."

He knew now. Before, he'd just suspected.

"One shot in the back, and one in the shoulder. Charles is right-handed," Faith said, "so I'm betting he dropped his weapon as soon as he took that hit in the shoulder."

Ethan nodded.

"I'm also guessing..." Another hard breath. "That Curtis Thatch didn't plan to let Charles—or any of you—walk out of that room."

"You're the up-and-coming D.C. detective," Ethan murmured. "Aren't you the one who is always figuring out how the criminals think? If you believe that was his plan..."

"Don't give me that crap. You don't need to sugarcoat with me."

"You're a cop. That means I always have to sugarcoat."

Her mouth tightened. "You know how I am, Ethan. No matter what happens, I try to be fair. Yeah, I might have spent some time trying to nail your ass to the wall, but I go by the book, always."

One of the things he respected about her. Staring into her eyes, Ethan said, "There were two reasons why I called you in from D.C."

Faith lifted a brow.

"First is family. Your family isn't as shit-twisted as mine, so I knew you would want to be there for Charles. Favorite cousin and all that..."

"How the hell long did you know he was FBI?" Faith demanded.

Seriously? "I knew day one. And really, you should have realized that. I have sources, and I'm sure no idiot." The fact that she thought he'd been in the dark so long was just insulting. "But I figured having an FBI agent as a guard could be a good thing. At least he wouldn't go crazy and try to kill me." *Like my last bodyguard.*

"Ethan..." A warning edge had entered her voice.

He ignored the warning. "You didn't answer my question before. Is your cousin okay?"

"Yes." For a moment, it almost seemed as if her eyes misted. "He'll be playing bench for the Bureau during the next few weeks, but he's going to make it. And I'm pretty sure I have you to thank for that, don't I?"

"No, actually, you need to thank Carly Shay. She's the one who stopped Curtis Thatch before he could fire again. And I want to be very clear, Curtis *was* going to fire again. He had that gun aimed, and he was just about to pull the trigger. My money says he was taking either a head or heart shot that time, but Carly stopped him. She tackled him. They both hit the floor, and Curtis lost that gun." His lips curled. "And Charles lived to play an undercover operative again another day."

She started tapping her foot. "You only listed one reason."

He waited. The bars were between them and no guards were in sight.

"What was the second reason you called me?"

"Carly Shay."

Her head tilted to the right as she studied him.

"You might just be the best cop I ever met." And he wasn't just trying to flatter her. "In terms of detectives I trust...hell, you *are* the one that comes to mind. You want me locked up because you think I'm a criminal."

"Uh, you *are*."

"But it's not political with you. You're not on the take. Never have been, and I don't think you ever will be."

She backed up a step. "You've had me investigated. *That's* how you knew my cousin was FBI."

His hands curled around the bars. "They aren't going to let me out of here. Charles heard me confess to crimes—well, let's just say my past will come to a most unsavory light. Even the strings I pulled before, they aren't going to save me. I'll go down, and when that happens, Carly will be alone."

She blinked at him. "You just said you knew I wasn't on the take—so why does it sound as if you're trying to set me up for some kind of bribe or—"

He laughed, cutting her off. "No bribe. Not you." His laughter died. They needed to be clear here. "I'm just talking about a payback. Carly was the one who saved Charles. Now I want you to help save her." He fought to keep the emotion out of his voice. Emotion wouldn't help any. "She can't be charged with crimes. Go talk to her. Convince her to make any deal she needs. Then help to get her some place safe."

Faith shook her head. "That's all above my paygrade, and you know it. I'm not Witness Protection or—"

"I know who your lover is, Faith. I know you and Will Hawthorne have been involved for a very long time, and I get why you don't go public. You don't want anyone to ever say you slept your way to the top, and honestly, anyone dumb enough to say that deserves to have the shit kicked out of them."

She swallowed.

"But Will Hawthorne has strings he can use." Hawthorne was a freaking powerhouse financially and politically. "And for you, he'd use them. He'd help to get her a new start, and you know it. She doesn't deserve to be hunted. She's a good person. Always has been. She just had the bad luck to get tangled up with bad things—" He broke off, laughing roughly. "Me. I was her bad thing." But he wouldn't be, not any longer.

"I don't understand you."

He shrugged. "Most people don't."

"Why do I get the feeling that Carly Shay does?"

Once more, he saw Carly as she'd been—on the floor, blood on her—Curtis's blood—and horror on her face. "Yes," he said, voice hard and gruff. "I think she does."

"I'll see what I can do." Faith turned away. She'd taken two steps when she stopped and glanced back. "Tell me that you've called Sophie."

"Worried about me?"

"You've *called* Sophie."

"There are some things that even Sophie can't fix." An FBI agent had heard his confession. And Carly had looked at him as if he were the devil himself. "I'm done."

She gave a low, long whistle, then headed out. The door groaned once more as she left.

He put his forehead on the bars and wondered how he'd gotten to this place. Had he always been destined for hell? Or had he just driven himself straight there without looking at other options?

Fuck it. Can't change the past. Can't change me. But Carly will be okay, and that is all that matters.

Carly.

***

Detective Faith Chestang pulled out her phone the minute she was outside of the PD. She had Sophie's telephone number in her contact list—okay, so *maybe* she and Sophie met for coffee once a week—and she dialed the other woman, fast.

When Sophie answered, Faith said, "I think Ethan Barclay has gone insane." Because unless she was wrong, it looked as if the guy wasn't going to fight any of the charges that could be pending against him. "You might want to get your butt on the next plane or train and get to NY."

Because Ethan was right about one thing— she was a good cop. And as a good cop, she wasn't going to just stand by and watch him crash and burn.

He'd killed Curtis Thatch, yes, but he'd done that while saving her cousin. And as for Quincy Atkins...

Word on the street was that a video tape had been recovered from Thatch's hotel room. A video that showed Quincy's murder.

She wanted to see that tape. So how was she going to get her hands on it?

***

Ethan was lying on the cot in his cell when he heard the groan of that door a few hours later. Footsteps headed toward him. Heavy. Hard.

Not Faith, her step was ever so much lighter.

He kept his eyes closed. The cell's lights had remained on as the day waned and night grew. An annoyance, but one that hadn't really bothered him. After all, sleep was the last thing he wanted.

In sleep, he feared the nightmares might come. Nightmares in which he didn't save Carly.

Sonofabitch.

"Aren't you going to say something, Agent Monroe?" Ethan finally murmured, still with his eyes shut. He could practically feel the other guy, standing just beyond his cell.

Then he heard another sound—the creak of a lock turning.

His eyelids flew up and he lurched to his feet. The cell door swung open.

"Yeah," Victor said. "You're free to go."

"Bullshit."

Victor just shrugged. "Your lawyer is finishing up the paperwork, and I'll need you in for a full recap of events tomorrow—"

"I haven't given *any* recap so far." This wasn't standard operating procedure. What the hell was happening? "I was just shoved in this hole and left here." The PD had taken over at the brownstone. They'd taken him to the police station, not to the FBI office, and he'd been locked away. *Forgotten?*

"Yeah, you were shoved in here, all right. That would be thanks to my order." Victor offered him a tiger's smile. "You're welcome."

Ethan grunted. "And now I get a free pass?"

"Nothing in this world is free, you should know that. But a man I respect—Charles West— he swore that you had no choice but to kill Curtis Thatch. And after I saw the little video of Quincy Atkins's murder…"

"So there really was a video?"

"You mean…*another* copy of the video, right? Because I believe you destroyed the original some time ago."

Ethan didn't reply.

Victor cleared his throat. "Any jury that sees that video won't convict you, and you know it. So maybe I could tie you up with an obstruction charge and unlawful body disposal—*if* I could even find the body."

No one would ever find that particular body.

"But then your lawyer—nice, lawyer, by the way—Sophie Sarantos is pretty much hell on wheels." Admiration lightened his tone.

Sophie? He met Sophie?

"But then your lawyer…" Victor said again, clearing his throat, "would just call up *my* FBI agent buddy to the stand, and then Charles would talk and tell the jury about how you and Carly Shay saved his ass." Victor exhaled on a long sigh. "And that's how you get a hung jury. Or maybe you get jury nullification—who knows which option they'd choose? Either way, you wouldn't go to prison and tax payers would be out a whole lot of money."

He was supposed to buy that the guy was just letting him walk? "Nothing in this world is free," Ethan said, giving Victor those same words back.

Victor looked toward the open cell door, then back at Ethan.

Ethan knew more was going on there—a whole lot that he didn't understand. He would, though, soon enough. For that moment...

He was getting his ass out of there.

Ethan took his time walking out of the holding area and through the station. Victor even gave him street clothes to change into—something damn else that he'd owe the guy for at a later date. And as he finally made his way through the bullpen, some cops stopped what they were doing and glanced his way.

That's right, boys and girls...the criminal walks.

Only they weren't looking at him with anger.

And Ethan got uncomfortable as he headed toward the door.

He stepped out into the New York night...

"I swear, your tab just keeps growing with me," Sophie Sarantos told him.

He turned to the side. She'd been standing in the shadows. Now she stepped forward into the light cast by a street lamp and waved her fingers at him. "Hi, there, Trouble."

"You got me out." Sophie was one of his oldest friends. And Victor had been right—one hell of a lawyer.

Sophie and Faith were opposites—he'd always thought so. Faith played down her attractiveness, but Sophie, well, she used it ruthlessly. Right then, she was dressed in a tight pencil skirt and a low cut top. Her dark hair tumbled over her shoulders and her golden skin—courtesy of her Greek ancestry—gave her an exotic flare beneath the harsh lights.

"I worked a little magic." She put her hand on his shoulder and steered him toward the waiting car. When he climbed inside, he wasn't particularly surprised to see Sophie's lover, Lex Jensen, behind the wheel. Lex glanced back at him, giving Ethan a long, unreadable stare.

Ethan sighed and leaned back against the leather seat. "You're not just going to drive me to some remote spot and dump my body, are you, Lex?" He closed his eyes, feeling weariness pull at him. But, instantly, Carly's face flashed in his mind's eye. Her face—her fear, her horror. Dammit.

"Tempting," Lex muttered. "But I think that's more your style."

True enough.

A car door slammed. "I heard that Lex," Sophie scolded. "I told you, play nice."

Ethan laughed. Lex might look like the typical American good-boy with his blond hair and pretty-boy face, but that guy could be as hard core as he wanted to be. Lex was part of VJS Protection, Inc., and that fellow played plenty rough when he wanted.

That roughness was why Ethan was glad the guy had wound up with Sophie. Ethan liked to know that his friend was safe, and with a fighter like Lex ready to destroy anyone who so much as looked the wrong way at her, well, Sophie was certainly safe.

The car accelerated as Lex took them to— well, wherever the hell they were going.

"Aren't you going to ask about her?" Sophie asked.

His jaw locked. "How did *you* find out I was locked up?"

"A trusted source."

"Your BFF—Faith, right?" Figured. Opposites with their clothes, but down deep, where it mattered—just alike. Fighters. And both with hearts that were too damn big. Hearts that could get them into trouble. No wonder they met weekly for their chat time—*like I don't know about that.* He made it a point to know everything that went down in D.C. And one thing he definitely realized—those two women got each other.

"Leave my BFF out of this." A light note had entered Sophie's voice. Odd, Sophie wasn't given to a lot of humor. Especially not on nights like this one. He cracked open one eye. They were moving fast through the city, and her face was in the shadows. "Ethan." The lightness faded from her tone. "Why aren't you asking about Carly?"

Because it hurts. "All I need to know..." Did he sound choked up? Hell, he *did*. He cleared his throat. Coughed. "I just need to know that she's somewhere safe."

Silence.

"Sophie..."

"She's safe, Ethan."

He nodded.

"What were you going to do?" Sophie wanted to know. "Trade your crimes—for her life? Offer a deal to the FBI?"

"It wasn't a bad plan."

"No, but not a good one, either. Speaking as your lawyer, it seriously sucked."

"Not if it got her safety in return."

They traveled more in silence.

"I've got you a room at a hotel," Sophie finally said. "The presidential suite, because I know how you like your comfort."

After living in squalor, yeah, he'd learned to appreciate fucking comfort. "When you have nothing," he said, knowing he was revealing too much with Lex there, but so what? Sophie had been with Ethan when he'd been in the gutter. "You want it all."

Only...what would he trade to have another chance with Carly? To have her not look at him as if he were a freak?

Worse...

A killer.

I am what I am.

Sophie pressed a keycard in his hand. "Floor thirty-six," she told him. "Get some sleep tonight, and I'll meet you in the lobby first thing tomorrow. The place has excellent security—"

"I made sure of that," Lex added.

"So you can rest without worrying. In the morning, we'll talk and I'll tell you everything I discussed with the cops."

The car had pulled to a stop. Weary now, Ethan just shook his head. "As long as you didn't sell my soul to them for my get-out-of-jail free card, I don't really care what you discussed with them."

He climbed from the car. She didn't follow him, but Sophie did reach out and grab his wrist. "I thought you'd lost your soul a long time ago."

He smiled at her. "I did. I gave it to a seventeen-year-old girl...a beautiful girl who was willing do to anything in order to save my sorry ass."

"Ethan..."

"Good night, Sophie. And don't worry, I'll pay you back for this."

He pulled away from her.

"No, Ethan, you won't. This time, I'm paying *you* back. We both know I owe you, far more than can be repaid."

Sophie—she'd always had a good heart. Lex had better treat her like the princess she fucking was.

Ethan headed into the swanky hotel. At this hour, the lobby was deserted. Good. Since the place was empty, no one gave him a second glance as he strode around the swank hotel in his loaner jeans and T-shirt.

He rode the elevator up. Stared at his bedraggled expression in the glass. Huh. How about that? He was definitely looking like more of a monster these days.

The elevator dinged when it hit the top floor. The lush carpet swallowed the sound of his footsteps. He used the keycard to enter the suite. It was dark inside. Not pitch black, though, because lights from the skyline spilled in from the floor to ceiling windows.

Those lights spilled in...and spilled on *her*.

Carly rose from the couch. She was wearing a light blue gown. She took a step toward him, her hands outstretched—

Ethan shook his head.

Carly froze.

"You aren't here." He shut the door behind him. Locked it. "You're some place safe. Sophie told me...you were safe."

Hesitantly, she advanced toward him. Her feet were bare and her hair slid over her shoulders. "I am safe, Ethan," she said. "I'm always safe with you."

She was less than a foot away. He could reach out and touch her. Instead, his hands balled into fists. "I tried to do one good thing. I tried again—for you."

"What did you try?" Her voice was soft. Husky. Tempting. He hadn't looked directly into her eyes, not yet. He was afraid of what he'd see.

"I tried to let you go." His voice was a stark contrast to hers. Rough and grating, and he wanted so badly to touch her. "Like before, I was going to stand back...you were going to walk away."

"But that's not what I want."

He stared over her shoulder. He couldn't look into her eyes, not then. "I saw, baby. Your fear and pain and—"

"I saw, too, Ethan. I saw that you'd do anything for me. Just as I would do anything for you. And I finally realized something I should have known long ago. I *saw* the truth that I missed before."

Don't look in her eyes, don't... "What was that?"

"You love me."

His gaze shot to hers. To her beautiful eyes. So deep. Deep enough that, hell, yes, he'd lost his soul to her years ago. His soul. His heart. Everything good.

"That's why you sent me away before, isn't it?" Carly asked.

He could be a coward and deny it. Or... "Yes." He wasn't a fucking coward.

"And that's why you were going to let me go again?"

"Yes." More a growl than anything else.

"I'd like to hear the words, Ethan."

"And I would like to strip you and fuck you right here." Each breath seemed to burn his lungs. "You know what I am. I'm not good. Not some fucking hero. I'm a killer. I've lied, I've stolen, and I've done anything and everything necessary for survival. But the worst part of me...it's the part that is so desperate for you. I see you, and I want. I want to take. I want to consume. I want to possess you forever. And that right there tells me that what I feel for you, it's all twisted up. It's wrong. It's not what you deserve and—"

"I would like to strip you and fuck you right here, too," Carly confessed, voice husky.

His heartbeat drummed, too fast. Too hard.

"And we will get to that," Carly promised. "But first, I want the words, Ethan," she said again. "I need to hear them."

Fuck it. "I love you."

Silence.

He should have said them...softer. Not snarled them. Or growled them or whatever the hell it had been that he'd done.

But—

Carly threw her body against his. She wrapped her arms around him and held on tight. "Again," she said.

His hands curled around her and he lifted her up, holding her easily as she locked her legs around his hips. "I love you."

She laughed, and it was a beautiful sound. So happy and free and he wanted to hear Carly laugh like that forever.

His heart was hurting. Beating too fast. Seeming to swell in his chest. Yes, dammit, yes, he did love her. Twisted and bent and as warped as he was, Carly was the one he loved.

Always.

Always had.

Always would.

He kissed her.

CHAPTER TEN

Her hands locked around Ethan's neck, and she pulled him closer. Carly put her mouth on Ethan's, so desperate for his kiss. She'd been waiting for him, sitting in the dark, each moment ticking by so slowly. Victor had advised her to stay away from the police station and when Sophie had appeared—she'd been adamant that Carly would be safer at the hotel's luxury suite. Apparently, the place had some kickass security that the staff used for those who stayed in that VIP area.

Carly had met Sophie, years ago. She'd always liked and respected the other woman, and she'd known that, if anyone could get Ethan out of police custody, it would be that lawyer.

"I...I'm not in control..." Ethan's voice was ragged. He took two steps and her back hit the wall. "Give me...moment..."

No, she'd waited long enough. She could feel the long, hard edge of his arousal pressing to her sex. He was kissing her now, frantically, and she met him eagerly. There would be no *moment*. There was just now. This. Them.

His hands were digging into her hips. Her breasts were aching, the nipples tight and hard as they thrust against his chest. The thin gown she wore provided very little coverage. When she'd wrapped her legs around him, the gown had hiked up and she could feel the air on her thighs.

A scrap of lace—her panties—was in the way. Her panties. His jeans. She needed those barriers gone so that Ethan could sink deep into her.

But he pulled his mouth away from hers. His breath sawed out in heavy pants. "Need...time..."

And she needed to be very, very clear with him. "I want you." She'd said that before. What was the guy missing?

But he gave a grim shake of his head. "You need care. Gentleness—"

Her nails raked down his back.

He hissed out a breath.

It wasn't going to work if he kept treating her like a victim—they weren't going to work. She wanted to kiss the past goodbye and move forward, full speed ahead. The best way to do that? Throw away the kid gloves. "Rip my panties out of the way, Ethan."

She felt his whole body stiffen.

"You said before that I had to tell you what I wanted." Her voice had gone husky. Could he hear her desire? She wanted him so badly. "I'm telling you. I want you to rip those panties out of the way."

Do it. Do...

His right hand slid around her hip. Down, down. She felt his fingers brush over her sex, caressing her through the lace of those panties. That one touch singed her, burning her whole body and making her ache even more for him.

"Rip—"

She heard the sound of those panties tearing, and then his fingers were on her. Stroking her sex. And she got wet for him, so very fast. Maybe she'd been wet and ready from the moment he started kissing her. He eased two fingers into her and Carly's eyes squeezed shut. *Yes, yes!*

But she didn't just want his fingers. "Un...unzip your jeans." She barely got those words out. Speech was about to be way beyond her.

His hand slid away and she heard the hiss of his zipper.

Then she felt the tip of his cock pushing into her. She gasped at the contact, and he stilled.

"Baby..."

Her eyes opened. She stared straight at him. "I'm not afraid. I want you. Don't hold back. *Don't.*"

This wasn't Quincy. This wasn't the past. This was their moment.

He sank into her and she moaned because he was what she'd needed. Exactly what she'd wanted so badly. Ethan withdrew, then thrust back into her. Her heels dug into his ass as she arched against him. Pinned between Ethan and the door, he controlled the thrusts, but she was squeezing him with her sex, arching, taking, and going insane with pleasure.

Skin to skin. There was no condom between them, and she loved feeling him that way. So hot and full. Each thrust sent him sliding over her clit and deep, deep into her. She put her mouth to his throat. Licked. Suck. Bit.

Her control was gone, and she wanted him just as desperate.

But...he was still holding back. Still trying to be so careful...

"Baby, protection, you need..."

She bit him again. "I'm covered and I'm clean."

"I-I'm clean, too. Don't take risks." His words were growled. "Never, but with you...fuck, with *you...I need more control. I should—*"

"You should fuck me harder." She clenched her sex around him. "Make me only think of you." And not blood or death or fear. No desperate worries that Ethan would be locked up and she'd never see him again. She didn't want to think about any of that. She just wanted him. Always, him.

He gave a ragged groan, and then his control did seem to break away. He drove into her even harder. Even deeper. Fast, strong thrusts. And he was kissing her neck now. Licking her. Giving her a light bite as her head tipped back against the wall. Pleasure rolled within her, rolling and rolling and—

Exploding. Igniting. Taking her over and all she could do was hold on tight for that wild ride with him. Hold on as the world spun out of control all around her.

Then she felt him—a hot splash inside of her as he came, and his body shuddered against hers.

She kissed him, wanting to taste his pleasure. Wanting to make the moment last just a little longer. Because when they were together like this—it truly was just them. Their own world. No one else.

Nothing else.

She heard the drumming of a heartbeat. Fast and deep. Hers? His? It didn't matter.

Her eyes opened, and Ethan was staring down at her. He was still in her, and her legs still had their death grip around his hips. Without a word, he started walking, holding her easily, staying buried inside of her, as he maneuvered through the suite.

"First door..." She licked her lips. Tasted him. "First door is the master bedroom."

And that door was conveniently open. He carried her inside. But he didn't head toward the bed. Instead, he went straight to the bathroom, and he lowered her to the tiled floor right in front of the massive, claw-foot tub. Her toes curled against the tile as he bent and a flick of his hand sent the hot water pouring into the tub. Steam rose a few moments later, and then Ethan stepped into the tub. He offered her his hand.

Her fingers curled around his, and she climbed in, too. They sank into the water, and he was behind her. Her back slid against his stomach, and the warm water surrounded her.

His arms wrapped around her. And he just—held her there.

Carly didn't think she'd ever felt safer in her life.

***

"Where is Ethan Barclay?"

Victor turned at the question. He was at the hospital, had just dropped by that morning to check in with Charles. But Charles's very fierce cousin had been on patrol, and Faith had only let him stay a few moments before telling him that visiting time was over—and that Charles needed his rest.

Apparently, Victor's FBI badge hadn't impressed the woman very much.

"Agent Monroe, *where is Ethan Barclay?*"

Victor's gaze sharpened on the man approaching him. Dr. Keith Nelson. Looking awfully hale and hearty, but still wearing a hospital ID bracelet, even though he was dressed in normal street clothes.

"Is he in custody?" Keith asked. "Have you arrested him for what he did to me?"

Right. He hadn't brought Keith up to speed yet. Mostly because time had passed in a wild blur. "The man who attacked you—the man I *believe* left you in Carly Shay's apartment—is dead."

Relief had Keith's shoulders slumping. "Thank God. I-I was discharged thirty minutes ago, and when I saw you here, I just had to stop and ask...I was afraid to go home thinking that Barclay might come after me..."

"The evidence I've collected didn't indicate that Ethan Barclay was your abductor."

"But—but I told you...he *threatened* me." Keith swiped a hand over his face.

Victor hesitated. "I was going to wait and have this talk down at the FBI branch. If you've been discharged, as you say...then how about we head to the Bureau's office?"

But Keith violently shook his head. "No, you tell me, *now*. Tell me what's going on! If Ethan Barclay didn't attack me, then who did?"

"I believe it was a man named Curtis Thatch."

Keith blinked.

"According to intel I'm still gathering, Curtis has actually racked up quite the body count. After abducting you, he also took Ethan Barclay. He planned to kill Ethan, but, well, Ethan had other ideas..."

Keith's shaking fingers rose and touched his temple. "Ethan killed him. He killed this—Curtis Thatch?"

"Yes, doctor. That's exactly what happened." His eyes swept over the shrink's face. "You look really pale to me. Are you sure that you have the okay to be discharged?"

Keith stumbled back. "I-I'm fine."

The guy didn't look so fine. "I want you to come with me," Victor said. "We'll talk at the Bureau office."

Keith's hand fell. "Where is Carly?"

"I'm not at liberty to say that right now."

Keith lunged forward and grabbed Victor's shirt. "*Is she all right?*"

Wow. The doctor seriously needed to calm the hell down. "Ease up. Just what meds did they give you in this place?"

Keith blinked, then he looked down at his hands—hands that had fisted Victor's shirt. "I just...with everything that has happened...all the time in the hospital...I started to worry."

"Right. Worrying about your patient's safety, that's normal and—"

"No." Keith's voice was a hoarse whisper. "I shouldn't say it...I shouldn't...confidentiality..." Then he began rubbing his temple again.

Alarms were going off in Victor's head. This guy—what was he holding back?

But then Keith squeezed his eyes shut. "Was she there when that man—that Curtis Thatch was killed?"

"Yes." He wanted to see where the doc was going with this bit.

Keith sucked in a sharp breath. "Then you need to bring Carly Shay in for an immediate psychiatric evaluation. The woman..." His eyes opened. "She could be on the verge of a psychotic break. She had one before, when she was seventeen years old. Carly Shay can be very, very dangerous, and for some time now, I've been concerned that she might be letting her...darker...urges take over."

"Carly Shay didn't kill Curtis Thatch." They should be clear on that. "And if you're saying she's some kind of imminent threat, if she's said something to you in a session that makes you believe she could be dangerous...then you *know* that is information that you should reveal to me. That's not protected by client privilege at all."

Keith glanced down at the gleaming floor.

"Has she?" Victor said, his voice snapping out. "Has Carly Shay ever said something to you that makes you believe the woman could have plans to kill?" He'd seen Carly as the victim. But...

"Yes," Keith admitted softly. "She has. And I'm afraid now...now she'll be pushed over the edge..."

***

Carly opened her eyes and saw the sunlight streaming through the window. She stretched, her body was full of delicious aches, and her hands brushed against Ethan's warm body.

Her head turned so that she could better see him. His dark hair was tousled, his tanned skin such a stark contrast to the white sheets. His eyes were closed, and she noticed just how incredibly long his lashes really were.

Her gaze slid over him. He was on his back, and the sheet had dipped low at his waist. She'd touched his scars last night—those on his stomach and chest. She'd felt them beneath her fingers, but, even when they'd been in the bath, the lights had been out so she hadn't seen them, not fully.

Now she did, and Carly felt tears sting her eyes. There were so many scars. Long and thick. Deep from the look of them.

Ethan had come very, very close to dying.

A tear slid down her cheek.

"Don't."

At his gravel-rough order, her gaze jerked back to his face. Only this time, his eyes were wide open and on her.

Ethan's hand lifted and his fingers slid over her cheek, catching the tear that had fallen there. "Don't cry for me, baby. The scars—they don't hurt."

"You almost died." But she wasn't just talking about the older attack by Daniel Duvato. She was talking about—dear God, had it just been yesterday? "You were in that chair, and he was going to kill you. If I—if I hadn't gone back to the brownstone..."

"Why did you come back?"

She drew in a shuddering breath. "Because I knew you hadn't left me. Victor was so sure you had, but it didn't fit. Not for us."

"You had faith in me." He seemed...surprised. Why?

Her body moved closer to his. "You think you're the only one who knows what love is, Ethan?"

His eyes widened. "What are you saying?"

"I'm saying...I should have taken you up on that offer sooner. Me and you, disappearing. Starting over. Letting the past go and moving on." *Seeing what a future together would be like.* "You're back in my life, and I don't want to let you go."

His eyes glinted down at her. "I want to hear the words, too."

She smiled. Smiling seemed to come so much easier to her, as long as Ethan was near. "I love you."

"Fuck yes." He dragged her closer and kissed her. Deep and hot and just the way she wanted.

She stretched against him, her body feeling so at ease with him. Everything was easy with him. It was—

Ethan had pulled away. He stared down at her for a moment, and his face hardened.

"What is it?" Carly asked him, hesitant now.

"I saw your face. When I killed Curtis, I saw you, baby."

She swallowed. Carly had known this would be coming, sooner or later. She'd rather hoped for later.

"How can you really love someone," Ethan began, voice slow, rough, "when you fear him so much?"

"Ethan..."

"I scare you."

She wasn't going to lie to him. If this was going to work, if they were going to work, there could be no lies. "Yes."

He flinched.

She kissed him. Hard. "That doesn't mean I can't still love you."

But he pulled away. He grabbed his jeans and jerked them on and marched toward the window.

"When you love someone..." His gaze was on the city. "That person is supposed to make you feel safe. Protected."

She wrapped a sheet around her body and sat on the edge of the bed. Carly wished they could go back to some cuddling. Maybe a little pillow talk. But they had to get past *this*. Or there wouldn't be any going forward for them. "You do make me feel safe."

He glanced back at her. "And I scare you to death."

"Violence scares me." She shot to her feet and confronted him, knowing exactly how important this moment was for them. "Seeing a man's throat get cut open, right in front of me, hell, yes, *that* shit scares me. If it didn't, I don't think I'd be normal."

He laughed. Bitterly. "We both know I'm not normal."

She grabbed his arms and let the sheet fall. So what if someone glanced up—way up—and caught a show? "Stop it."

A furrow appeared between his brows.

"Stop always playing the bad guy. I get that you like the role, but with me, leave it at the door."

His eyes widened.

"I know what you're capable of doing, Ethan. I know better than just about anyone. And you really want to know what scares me most about you? It's not the violence because I know you would never hurt me. That's not who you are. But...I know...*I know* just how far you'd go for me. I know you'd fight, you'd kill—" A hard smile curved her lips. "And I know you *have* done all of that, for me. To protect me. And it scares the hell out me, knowing that I'm the one who pushes you so far."

He didn't say anything.

She realized her nails were digging into his arm. "Do I push you *too* far?" Because that was her fear. For her, he'd do anything. Even lose his soul in order to keep her safe.

She knew there were no lines he wouldn't cross.

For me.

That knowledge did scare her.

Because, deep inside, she had long ago realized her dark truth, too. For Ethan, there were no lines that she wouldn't cross.

"You don't push me," Ethan said, voice sounding almost rusty. "You...make me feel whole. When I didn't even know that part of me was missing."

She stood on her tip-toes and brushed a gentle kiss over his cheek. "We can make it," she whispered. "I know we can."

Because she didn't want to be with anyone else. Sure, she'd survive without Ethan, but she wouldn't be happy. And there would always be that empty spot inside of her, a spot he'd claimed in her heart so long ago.

"I would do anything for you." His words were a confession, and she realized that. "No laws I wouldn't break. No sins I wouldn't commit. Can you really live with that?"

"Ethan—"

A phone rang. She glanced around, the sound oddly jarring, and then she saw Ethan's phone on the floor.

They should ignore the call. Just forget it, but...

But we nearly died yesterday. What if that's the FBI? What if something else happened?

She was the one who grabbed his phone. And she saw Sophie's picture on the screen. She handed the phone to Ethan, suddenly becoming highly conscious of her nudity.

Ethan didn't answer the phone. His fingers curled around it, but he kept staring at Carly. "Can you live with what my love means? Can you live with *me*?"

The phone stopped ringing.

"I don't want to try living without you again." She'd meant exactly what she'd said before. "I love you, Ethan. And I can handle your darkness." She wasn't saying it would be easy. But the one man on earth who made her feel protected and cherished—it was the one man she'd seen kill.

Twisted? Insane?

Maybe.

But maybe not.

"Can you handle mine?" Carly asked him.

His phone started ringing again. She looked at the screen. She could see Sophie's face once more.

"Something could be wrong," Carly said. "Answer it."

His gaze was still on her. "You don't have a darkness, baby. You have light. A bright, fucking shining light that makes my whole world better. And if anyone else says different, I will kick their asses."

The phone stopped ringing.

"I don't want to scare you again," he rasped, "but, baby, you always come first for me. Your safety—that's it for me. If you're put at risk, you know how I'll respond."

She did. And it was the same way that she would respond.

Someone started pounding on the door then. They both turned at once, and Ethan rushed from the bedroom. She grabbed for her discarded gown and yanked it over her head. She hurried after him—

The suite's door was shoved open before Ethan could reach it.

She caught sight of Victor Monroe. Behind him stood a guy who appeared to be a hotel employee—based on his uniform. And—Sophie was there too, crowding in with the men.

"What the hell?" Ethan snarled. "I was coming to the damn door! You didn't have to bust in!" He glared at them. "What did you think, I was attacking her in here?"

The hotel employee still had a keycard in his hand. He yanked the keycard back and leapt behind Sophie.

Victor stepped into the suite. His gaze went first to Ethan, then to Carly. "Actually, I thought it might be the other way around."

"What?" Ethan shook his head.

"I thought..." Victor continued as he advanced. Only he wasn't advancing toward Ethan. He was closing in on Carly. "I thought she might try to hurt you."

Goosebumps covered her at those words.

"Hold the hell up," Ethan said, raising his hand. "You were worried about me? *Me?*" He laughed. "Sweet. Really, touching, agent, but—"

Victor's jaw hardened. "Look, asshole, it goes with the badge, okay? You find out that someone could be in danger, you react."

Ethan's gaze raked him. "You seriously think I'm in danger, from Carly?" He waited a bit, then bluntly stated, "Not happening."

"I don't think..." Victor began carefully as his gaze slipped to Carly. She felt far too exposed in her gown. "I don't think you know her as well as you believe."

Ethan stepped in front of her, shielding Carly with his body. "I know her plenty well." He glanced back at her. "Baby, why don't you go get dressed? I've got this guy."

She started to back away.

"You have a history of hurting men, don't you, Ms. Shay?" Victor asked, his voice ever so careful. Almost...sad.

She stopped retreating. After all, there were some things that she couldn't run from in this world. Carly knew that now. She stepped around Ethan and she caught a glimpse of Sophie's worried face. The other woman moved forward quickly and caught Ethan's hand. "The next time I call you," Sophie snapped. "Answer the phone!"

Victor's voice had been soft, but Sophie's was hard with an edge—of worry.

This isn't good.

Ethan pulled away from Sophie and focused on Victor once more. "What's going on? I told you I'd come in today to answer your questions and sign your damn paperwork."

"I'm not here for you." Victor crossed his arms over his chest and his expression hardened even more. "This time, I came for Carly. It's over, ma'am. Your shrink talked. I know your secrets, and I know just what you've done." Again, his voice wasn't rough, even though his face sure was. He was talking softly to her, and Carly thought that she saw a flash of pity in his eyes.

He was doing his job, but the guy didn't like it.

A shudder worked over Carly's body. "No."

"I want you to come downtown with me."

She shook her head. "No, you've got it wrong. I-I don't know what Dr. Nelson told you—"

"I have to admit, when I first saw the video of Quincy's death, I totally bought that you were a victim, but then the shrink started talking, telling me about what you'd threatened, about the men you'd hurt."

The men she'd—

"You don't like for your lovers to get too clingy, do you? When they push for too much, when they push for what you don't want them to have...you turn on them."

It was hard to breathe. "Stop." This wasn't happening.

But Victor didn't stop. He continued, in that soft, almost sympathetic voice. "That's what the doctor said about you. He said you confessed all in your sessions."

She hadn't. Not to Nelson. She'd always been careful with him. Hadn't that been one of the reasons she terminated therapy? If you couldn't share openly with a shrink, what was the point? And she'd shared so very little in her sessions with him because he'd made her feel so on edge.

Victor turned his attention to Ethan. "Did you know that she was put in a psychiatric hospital when she was seventeen, after she took a knife and attacked a twenty-one year old man named Jon Mathers?"

Jon's image flashed in her mind.

Carly shook her head once, violently. "Nelson shouldn't have...told you that."

"She was deemed to be a threat to others, so she was locked up." Victor squared off with Ethan. "Did you *know* that about her? Because I don't think you did. I don't think you knew that they had to restrain her because she kept attacking the staff in that facility. That they had to strap her down and drug her because she was so dangerous."

Ethan's face bleached of color. He shoved Victor out of his way. "Carly?"

She blinked, refusing to let any tears fall from her eyes. "I didn't want you to know..."

"She was a victim," Sophie fired at the FBI agent. "Of course, it stands to reason that she had an episode after the attack by Quincy. I don't even know the particulars of that case with Jon Whatever-His-Name was, but I'm betting it was probably some guy who got a little too handsy with her. He gave her a flashback to her attack..."

Everyone knows now. Everyone.

"And she snapped. She reacted. I've seen other abuse victims respond the same way. It's *survival.*" Fury dripped in Sophie's voice. "And you, *Agent Monroe,* should know better. You should—"

"I did think the same thing, ma'am. At first. I've been in this business a long time, and I've seen a lot of shit go down." Victor's breath expelled in a low rush. "And, unfortunately, one of the things I've seen is that victims...they can be changed. Their pain makes them into something new. Predators."

"I'm not," Carly whispered.

"*Defending* yourself doesn't mean you're a predator!" Sophie threw at him.

"No, but targeting other prey does." Victor rocked back on his heels. "Dr. Nelson has been tracking Carly, since she became his patient. He discovered three other men that Carly dated...men who have since gone missing over the years."

Ethan had moved closer to her. He lifted his hand and touched Carly's cheek. "I should have been with you."

"*Tracking* her?" Sophie repeated. "Did you say Nelson was *tracking* her? That sounds obsessed to me. I think you need to—"

"I checked out his story. Those men *have* vanished. Without a freaking trace. And their only link is Ms. Shay here. According to her shrink, she admitted to wanting to hurt those men. Wanting them to feel part of the pain she carried."

Carly shook her head again. "That's not true."

"I know," Ethan said, his voice soft.

"I didn't mean to hurt him," Carly said, wanting Ethan to understand this. "Jon was kissing me. I was at a restaurant. Just...just lost. I told him to let me go. H-he didn't. No one was going to take from me again. No one would do what...Quincy did."

Ethan nodded. "You just made him stop."

She'd grabbed the knife from a nearby table. It had just been...*in my hand.* "I swiped out so he would stay away. I sliced his arm. People were screaming. And then I was locked up."

Locked up and crying for Ethan.

But she hadn't broken in that psych ward. She'd found herself. She'd realized that she was *never* going to let anyone lock her up again. She'd be in control. She would survive, on her own.

And she had.

Yes, she wanted to be with Ethan. But it was *her* choice. She could live without him. She wouldn't wither and die, but she *wanted* to be with him. She was happier with him. He helped her to hope.

My choice. Always.

"I'm sorry," Ethan said as his hand dropped. "Baby, if I could change things, if I could go back—"

She caught his hand. "Back is the last place I want to go. Forward. Only forward. With you."

He stepped closer to her. The heat of his body wrapped around her.

"Uh, yeah…" Victor mumbled. "This scene is touching, and honestly, with every bit of info I uncover, I do think you two make a crazy, but…probably fitting couple." He cleared his throat. "But I need you down at the station, Ms. Shay. Three men are missing, and your shrink says you confessed to wanting to—"

"No." Her voice was flat, almost calm, and she was proud of that fact. "I told Dr. Nelson that those men didn't click for me. That I couldn't feel comfortable around them. I couldn't let go with them. I *never* said I wanted to hurt them. Not them or anyone else. And as far as me being obsessed with someone from my past…" *Confess all.* "I don't think it was obsession. When I was seventeen, I was in love with Ethan. I thought I'd moved on, but then he came into my life again, and those feelings came back, too. Only stronger than before." Her shoulders were up, her spine straight. "I don't know why Nelson is telling you these lies, but that's what they are—lies. Am I dangerous? Yes, actually, I am. To anyone who tries to hurt me or the people I care about. But am I some kind of—of predator? No. No, I'm not." Her toes curled against the thick carpet. "Now, if you'll excuse me for a moment, I'm going to get dressed. Then I will come downtown with you. I want to see Nelson. I want to find out just why the hell he's lying about me."

She turned on her heel and walked very slowly back into the master bedroom. Carly shut the door behind her with a soft click.

And she still didn't let those tears fall.

CHAPTER ELEVEN

"Bullshit," Sophie called flatly when the bedroom door shut behind Carly. "This whole thing is bull, and I can't believe you actually bought it for even a moment, Agent Monroe."

Ethan made himself look away from that shut door and over at Victor. "You came to save my ass?" He gave the other man a tiger's smile. "Said it before, but I have to say it again. Sweet, bro. Sweet."

Victor growled back, "I had to follow up, okay? A threat was reported, and that woman in there—hell, yeah, I get it, she looks like a wet dream but—"

"Don't." That one word was low and lethal. Ethan's hands had fisted. "Don't talk about Carly like that. Don't fucking get her in your head that way at all."

Victor lifted his hands. "Easy. I just meant—I could see where a man—even you—would be taken in. I thought she was innocent, too, and—"

"She is innocent. Carly is *good*. The one good thing I have always had, the one thing I've tried to protect, but I screwed up, again and again."

Victor's expression was grim. "I've seen too many people be taken in during my time. Trust shouldn't come so easily."

"Maybe it doesn't come easily for you, but for me, with her—it does."

"Three men are missing."

"She's not involved."

Victor swore. "What? Are murders so commonplace for you that this crap doesn't faze you?"

Ethan just stared back at him.

"Fuck me." Victor backed up a step as his brow furrowed. "Am I looking at this all wrong? You're the one who made Quincy Atkins disappear, and then you're the one who rushed back into Carly's life. She didn't go looking for you. You came after her."

Ethan knew where the dick was going even before Victor said—

"How do you feel, knowing that Carly slept with those other men? Were you watching all those years? Keeping tabs on her? Going insane with jealousy when others got too close?" He waited a beat, then demanded, "Are *you* the reason those men disappeared?"

Before Ethan could say anything, Sophie jumped between him and the agent. "All right, Agent Jump-to-Conclusions," she said, voice sharp. "Calm down. You say you have proof these men are missing? First and foremost, I want to know *when* they vanished. Because I'm betting my *clients*," and she definitely emphasized the "*s*" on that word, "have alibis. This is some kind of witch hunt, and I don't like it."

"Dr. Nelson is the witness here. He's the one talking and pointing me right at your *clients*."

"Then I want to talk with him," Sophie said.

Victor laughed. "You know that isn't how it works. He's in protective custody right now. And he'll stay that way, until I get this mess sorted out."

The bedroom door opened. Ethan glanced back and saw that Carly was there, dressed in hip-hugging jeans and a loose top. "There isn't anything to sort out," she told him, obviously having overheard Victor's last comment. "I think it's clear what is happening here."

So did Ethan.

"My shrink wants you to think that I'm a killer. The same shrink who tried to get you to believe that Ethan was the man who'd abducted him. So for me," Carly said, nodding briskly, "that's twice he's lied. Twice he's tried to throw us under the bus, and I'd really like to know *why* he's done it."

It was one of those old school, *who do you believe situations?*

Only this time, an FBI agent had to decide...

"Do you trust the doctor?" Ethan asked. And he gave Victor a cold smile. "Or the killers?"

"Fuck me," Victor said again.

Exactly.

***

Carly's hands were clammy. Her heart raced too fast, and she was worried that her expression revealed too much.

"It's all right." The reassurance came from the man beside her, surprising Carly. Victor stood at her side, and for the briefest moment, his fingers brushed over her arm. "I'm going to be with you the entire time."

That had been the plan, anyway. A crazy plan that she'd agreed to because her life was on the line again, and she wasn't going to let anyone destroy her future.

My choice.

She'd made a choice when she came out of that suite. A choice to go down fighting.

The light outside of the hotel was incredibly bright as she left the building. Victor was a step in front of her. Ethan—Ethan was still inside the hotel. He was going to follow behind her with Sophie.

Before anything else happened, Victor had wanted Carly to have the chance to speak with his superiors. By going in—willingly—he'd said that she had a greater shot at getting folks to believe her because it would look as if she were cooperating.

Hell, she wasn't even sure if Victor believed her. He'd certainly been suspicious enough when he first stormed in the suite. But now...now he at least *seemed* to be giving her the benefit of the doubt, softening some.

She hurried down the hotel's back steps and saw Victor's SUV waiting. The windows were dark, tinted.

He opened the passenger side door for her.

The bullets didn't make a sound when they fired. They erupted out of the gun and slammed into Victor, jerking his body back, one hitting after the other, and Carly heard herself scream when he fell.

But then she was staring down at that gun—a gun equipped with a silencer. A gun pointed straight at her as Dr. Keith Nelson smiled at her. "Get into the vehicle. Fucking now."

No, if she got into the vehicle...

"You can die right here. I will shoot you now and still get paid just as much money."

She'd screamed, but no one had come to her aid—it was too early, no one was out on the streets—and his finger was already starting to squeeze the trigger. She couldn't get in that SUV, and she couldn't let Victor die. He was still breathing. Carly could see the rise and fall of his chest. She had to get help for him.

Turning, she started to run away—

And a bullet hit her, slamming into Carly and sending her tumbling right into the cement. For a moment, she lay there, stunned, the pavement biting into her palms, her shoulder burning. She heard the rush of footsteps coming toward her. Carly pushed up to her knees, needing to run, but there wasn't time.

Hard arms grabbed her, wrenching her shoulder and making the white-hot pain flare even hotter. She cried out and tried to fight, but Dr. Keith Nelson was much stronger than he'd appeared to be. He dragged her toward the SUV, stumbling over Victor's sprawled body. She screamed, but no one was there. Still, *no one*. Victor had taken her out of building's back entrance, and no one could see, no one—

"*Carly!*" That roar was Ethan's. Her head wrenched toward his roar.

He was running toward her. But Keith had tossed her into back of the vehicle. Keith slammed the door, and she tried frantically to open it, but something was wrong. The handle was jammed.

She stared through the glass. Saw Ethan running toward her, with Sophie steps behind him. *That had been the plan. Ethan and Sophie were going to follow us to the Bureau. They were coming down on the next elevator. Everyone should have been safe.*

There was no safety. Because she saw—

She saw...she saw Keith lift his gun. He fired. Once. Twice. Three times.

She screamed again as both Ethan and Sophie hit the cement.

Then Keith ran around to the front of the SUV. He jumped into the driver's seat. She lunged for him, determined to stop him before he could start that vehicle and take her away.

Her nails scratched across his face.

"Dammit, you bitch, stop!" He whirled and brought the butt of the gun down against her temple. For an instant, the world dimmed. "You'd better be worth this fucking pay-off..."

She pushed up, ready to attack him again.

But the butt of the gun hit her once more. Even harder this time. The world didn't dim.

It went black.

***

As soon as the bullets stopped flying, Ethan jumped to his feet. He reached for Sophie, checking her out.

"I'm all right! I hit the ground as soon as he aimed the gun at me," she said. Then, before she could add anything else, Lex was running around the side of the hotel and charging right toward them.

Lex grabbed Sophie, pulled her close—

Right. She's good. I need Carly. Ignoring the pain in his arm—a damn bullet had grazed him— Ethan ran after the SUV. The bastard was driving it hell fast, careening down the street. Taking Carly away with him.

He'd been waiting. The freak must have followed Victor here, then he just slipped in Victor's vehicle and waited for the perfect opportunity to strike.

Keith Nelson's attack made sense if...*fucking hell.* Maybe Keith had never been attacked by Curtis Thatch. Maybe the two men had been working together all along.

Sonofabitch.

Hard fingers locked around Ethan's ankle, jerking his attention down and to the injured agent.

Victor looked like hell, his skin ashen, but he had a determined glare on his face as he said... "SUV...equipped with...GPS locator..."

Ethan smiled down at him. Hell, yes.

"Get...bastard..." Victor gasped. "Get...him..."

He would. The agent could count on that.

***

When she opened her eyes, Carly was being dragged out of the back seat. Keith was leaning over her, sweat streaming down his face, his hair tousled, his breath heaving—

She lifted her feet and drove them into his stomach, as hard as she could.

He let her go—immediately, and she fell straight onto the concrete. The impact jarring, knocking the breath right from her, but she rolled over and started to crawl away from him.

"Carly..." His voice seemed to echo and she realized they were in a cavernous parking garage. And they seemed to be the only people there. "I get paid if you're delivered alive or dead."

She stopped crawling.

"It's more, of course, if you're alive. There's a bonus payment then because there are buyers out there willing to make sure you suffer."

Carly could hear him walking closer.

"But one million to deliver your dead body? That's still one real nice piece of change."

She glanced over her shoulder. The gun was in his hands again.

If she tried to run, he'd shoot her. Even if the bullet didn't kill her, another injury would slow her down and could make escape impossible.

Think. Think.

Taking her time, she turned over and stared up at him. Slowly, she lifted her hands, her pose one of surrender.

"Good decision." His left hand rubbed his stomach. She hoped she'd given him bruises. Some internal damage would be awesome. "Carly, Carly, Carly...Do you know how many times I thought about killing you?"

Staring at him made her skin crawl.

"You were always so cautious with me. And a few times, I caught you staring at me, as if...you knew." He was right over her now. "But you didn't know, did you? No one ever sees past the mask. No one knows..."

"That you're a killer?" She thought that crap was pretty evident. "Uh, newsflash..." Her right arm was soaked with blood, her shoulder wound still throbbing. "You just shot an FBI agent. Witnesses were at the scene. *Everyone* is going to know what you are."

He knelt in front of her. The silencer was still on the gun and he slid it across her cheek. "I spent years listening to criminals. Learning their secrets. Hearing them brag about their crimes and show no remorse whatsoever. And do you know what I learned?"

She didn't really care. She just had to figure out a way to get that gun away from him.

"I learned that the criminals, the killers...they're the strong ones. What good is regret? Remorse? Our world truly is survival of the fittest, and if you're not fit, then you're just a waste of air."

This jerk had been her shrink?

"I adapted. I changed. I learned that their secrets were assets, and I sold them to the highest bidder."

Things started to click for her. If he'd been selling secrets... "You're the one who contacted Curtis Thatch. There was never...any abduction. He didn't take you. You—you were working with him!"

He shrugged. The gun was still at her cheek. "I thought my bruises and the scrapes were a nice touch. Told old Curt that it had to look legit. Then I just kept Ethan busy so that he wouldn't see Curt sneaking up behind him. Voila. Perfect plan. Curt was out of the way, and you—well, I was going to get my delivery check for offering you up *and* giving Curt the perfect means to punish you."

She shook her head.

He sighed. The gun moved away from her cheek. "*Ethan.* A man you actually cared about. See, Curt had already killed the others, but you didn't even know that. No, you didn't *care.* I brought the guys up to you in session, and you barely blinked. They didn't matter to you. I don't think anyone really mattered, except Ethan Barclay. When I saw you two together, when I watched from my window and saw you hug him so tightly, as if you couldn't bear to let him go, I immediately called Curt to let him know the perfect tool to torture you was at hand."

They'd planned to kill Ethan, in order to break me.

"Curt was all about the torture."

And you're all about talking. Arrogant asshole. But keep it up. Every second that passed...that was an opportunity for help to arrive. Ethan would come for her. She'd found him. He would find her. Carly didn't doubt that for a moment.

"People kill for so many reasons. Passion. Greed. But the kills that interest me the most...it's the kills that are for pleasure." He smiled down at her. "Curt was a connoisseur. Most of his kills were for pure pleasure, but you—you were for revenge. Payback. So he changed his MO. Took out men instead of women. Killed them quickly because it wasn't their deaths that mattered so much...but what he hoped the murders would do to you."

And I didn't even notice. Guilt tore through her, and she gagged because—three men were dead.

"Tage Price. Josh Lavelle. Ace Patton." Keith seemed to relish saying their names. "Men who paid the price because they tried to love you."

Her eyes squeezed shut as their images flashed through her mind. They'd been good men, all of them. They'd treated her well. They'd had families. Friends. Lives.

Lost.

"Curt made the bodies vanish. Seemed fitting. After all, that was what you did to his brother."

Her eyes opened. She swallowed back the nausea and tried to push the images—Tage, Josh, and Ace—from her mind. "Go screw yourself." *He* was responsible for those deaths. Keith and Curt. Twisted freaks.

She pushed up to her feet. Her body wavered, just a bit.

Then she tensed because she could hear the sound—the sound of an approaching car. Coming closer and closer in that parking garage. Hope filled her.

Keith's head tilted, as if he'd heard the sound too, and then he laughed. "Curt wasn't my only interested buyer. Quincy Atkins had allies, plenty of people who want to see his killer bleed. Some of them thought that Ethan was untouchable, but you—you can be touched plenty."

The sound of that car was getting closer. Keith didn't appear at all worried.

"That's my buyer. He's bringing me so much money for you. He'll take you away, and you won't ever be seen again. I'll vanish, as well. Who knows?" He smiled. "Maybe I'll try some pleasure killing, too. Curt always told me that the rush was truly incredible."

She had to run. There was an elevator waiting about thirty feet away. She could get there. Get the doors open—

"Ethan won't ever find your body. Maybe he'll think that you're alive. Maybe he'll hold out hope for a while. A month. A year. Maybe longer. But eventually, the truth will hit him." Keith gave a brisk nod. "And *you* set this all in motion. You wrapped your hands around *him,* right on the street. You weren't afraid of him. You wanted him. So plain to see. And I knew right then—Curt had his weapon. He could finally hurt you the way that he wanted."

"H-how did you become my shrink?" It made no sense that she'd wound up with this sick bastard.

"Oh, you mean, why did Dr. Hendricks recommend me to you before she left town? I actually helped her to leave. You see, I discovered some of her secrets, too. An addiction in her past that she wanted to stay hidden. To keep my silence, she sent you my way." He shrugged. "I told you, secrets really are my business."

The car came around the curve, shooting off the ramp that led to their level in that garage, heading straight for them.

Keith turned toward the vehicle, a smile on his face.

And that was her moment. His distraction. Her opportunity. She turned and ran, going as fast as she could toward that elevator.

"No!" Keith bellowed.

She didn't stop. She expected to feel another bullet hit her. So she started to zig and zag. Wasn't the advice that you were supposed to go all serpentine? Because bullets followed a straight trajectory, but people didn't have to?

Car doors slammed.

And—

Gunfire. Bullets booming and echoing around her.

But Keith had a silencer on his gun.

Her hand slammed into the elevator button.

She looked back, a desperate glance.

Keith was on the ground.

A woman—African American, with dark hair pulled back into a bun and a fierce glare on her delicate face—stood over Keith, her gun still trained on him.

But that woman wasn't alone.

Ethan was there, and he was running toward Carly.

The elevator doors opened, but she didn't move.

He found me.

"Move," the woman standing over Keith barked, "and you will get a bullet between your eyes."

Carly stumbled toward Ethan. He caught her and held tight. The sound of sirens reached her ears, safety—coming.

But I'm already safe. I'm with Ethan.

No, no—a buyer was coming. They were both still in danger. She shoved at his arms. "Keith had plans—another man was coming. To—to buy me and—"

"He's already in custody. Cops caught him outside. He pulled up right when Detective Chestang and I did."

Detective Chestang? The name was oddly familiar.

He threw a quick glance over his shoulder. "Faith is from D.C., but turns out she has a few friends on the Force in this area, too. Victor told us about the GPS tracker on his SUV, so it was easy for Faith and I to assemble a team and find Keith."

He'd worked *with* the cops?

"I was scared," Ethan confessed.

Cop cars swarmed behind him. Keith was still on the ground.

"He took you away from me." Ethan's hold tightened on her. "And I just had to get you back."

She could feel the strong, fast beat of his heart against her. He held her so tightly, so close but... "It hurts," Carly had to say.

He immediately let her go, then his gaze swept over her, locking on her blood-covered arm and shoulder, then coming back up to stare at her face—no her temple. Was her face as swollen as it felt? That gun butt to the head had hurt like hell.

Ethan scooped her into his arms and started running for the cops. Funny. Ethan, making that move. *Going to the cops.* If she didn't watch it, he'd be a regular boy in blue soon.

"I'm okay," she said, but she let her eyes close. She could do that now. Let the pain take over and just drift away. Ethan was there. Keith had been stopped.

He found me.

"No more, Carly. No more enemies coming out of the wood work. This shit has to stop."

She heard another blast of a siren. Her eyes cracked open and she spied an ambulance rushing toward her, hurtling around the curve in that parking garage. "Easier said...than done." Because soon, her story would be leaked even more. The FBI knew all about her past and with that Quincy death video being uncovered...anyone who wanted vengeance for Quincy's kill would be looking her way. Would a line form? And what was she supposed to do then?

"I won't let anyone hurt you," he said. His lips pressed to hers. "I'm done, baby. Done."

He wasn't. They weren't. Ethan had plenty of enemies on his own. His enemies. Her enemies. How were they ever supposed to find a safe place? How were they supposed to have a future?

The one thing she wanted so badly. A chance. Hope.

It was being taken away.

A tear slid down her cheek as Ethan lowered her onto the gurney. They had to find a way out of this mess.

What way was there?

Ethan's hand slid over her cheek. "Baby, I mean it. I'm done."

Her lashes lifted. She saw the forms of two EMTs as they rushed around her, checking her wounds. Someone shone a really bright-ass light into her eyes.

Then she was being lifted again. Put into the back of the ambulance. Ethan started to follow, but an EMT put a hand on his chest and shoved him back.

Bad move.

Ethan looked at the guy. Just looked.

The EMT hurriedly moved away. "My bad. Family, right?"

No. Yes.

Ethan climbed in the ambulance. He caught her hand in his. "Right. Family. You always have been mine, baby. Always will be."

The back doors shut. The ambulance lurched away.

***

The perp was laughing. That high-pitched, grating laughter was getting on Faith Chestang's last nerve. She glared at the guy and thought—oh, but another shot would have been good.

She'd already fired two bullets at the guy. When she'd arrived on scene, he'd been aiming at Carly's fleeing back. Ethan—acting in a seriously *un*-Ethan-like way—had jumped into the line of fire. Carly hadn't glanced back, so she hadn't seen him leap in front of Dr. Keith Nelson's gun.

Faith had seen the move, though. And before Keith could take out Ethan, she'd fired.

I saved Ethan Barclay's ass. Now he owes me. Plenty.

She'd call in her debt, too.

FBI agents and NYPD officers were everywhere. They all sure seemed pumped. Probably because they'd stopped a killer *and* arrested one of the FBI's most wanted—drug lord named Henry Hastings, a fool who'd been outside, heading into that garage with a trunk full of money.

He came to kill Carly.

Seemed plenty of people were offering a price on Carly's head.

That price would only vanish, once Carly was dead.

Luckily, Ethan had a plan to protect Carly. On their fast and frantic drive over, Ethan had told Faith all about that plan.

Some men would really do anything for love.

The stories she'd heard about Ethan were wrong. The guy did have a heart. It had just been buried deep, for a long time.

"So what the fuck is going to happen now?" Keith demanded. "You think you saved Carly Shay? The hits will just keep coming. They won't stop—"

"Don't worry about her. Worry about yourself." She smiled at him. The EMTs were loading him into a second ambulance. "What do you think is going to happen to you? Do you really think Ethan is going to let you get away with what you've done?"

Keith paled. "I've got...powerful friends..."

"So does Ethan. If I were you, I'd be praying right about now. Because you're under arrest, *doctor*. You're going to jail—or maybe hell. Guess they could be one and the same to you. And when you get there...I wonder how long you'll stay alive? The last enemy that Ethan had...Daniel Duvato...he didn't make it more than a few months..."

The EMT pushed on Keith's wound. The man howled.

"Better get used to pain," Faith advised him. "Something tells me that you'll have a whole lot more of it coming your way."

CHAPTER TWELVE

Two weeks later...

"I'm not the type of man who runs from anything or anyone."

Carly glanced over at Ethan. They were at his home in D.C. The last two weeks had pretty much been a whirlwind. She'd gotten stitched up at the hospital, she'd found out that Agent Victor Monroe had survived, and then...

Then she'd had to deal with the fallout.

She'd given a full statement to the FBI, with Sophie at her side. She'd admitted to killing Quincy, even though Sophie had said that *technically*...Ethan had dealt the killing blow.

Ethan hadn't given a statement, but he had gone through several closed-door meetings with FBI Brass. He hadn't wound up in jail after those meetings, but she was still afraid.

Worried their enemies would keep coming.

"I don't run," he said. "Not usually. But for you, baby, I'd do anything."

He eased down onto the couch beside her. "The FBI has offered to set us up with new identities. New names, a new place. And one hell of a lot less looking over our shoulders for our enemies to come calling."

Her breath caught. "You'd...do that?"

"I told you before...I'm done. Done with risking you. Done with anything that will put you in harm's way. You want a new life? I can give it to you. Just say the word, and it will happen."

Her heart raced too fast. "I do want a new life."

He nodded. "Then we'll leave tonight. You won't need to ever be afraid again and—"

"I want a life with you. I don't really care where we are. I just want you with me."

His gaze searched hers.

"You aren't the type of man to run," Carly said.

"I am if it means keeping you safe."

She had to know this. "How many others will come after us?"

"That drug lord Hastings was the last ally that Quincy had. Despite the bullshit Nelson was spouting, there are no other threats from that end. Hastings and Curtis were it, and they've been eliminated. Curtis is in the ground, and as for Hastings, the Feds discovered enough evidence in his car and on his laptop—fool had it with him in the trunk—to lock him away for the next fifty years." He shrugged. "Maybe...I helped a bit with that discovery. I might have known where Hastings had hidden some secrets."

She'd just bet that he had.

His fingers slid over her shoulder. She had a
scar there, one still bright red. It would fade over
time, but the memory would always be there.
Death, coming too close.

"The life I've built isn't an easy one. It's built
on danger and death and too many lies." He
nodded. "Maybe it's time to move on. Maybe it's
time to find more. I'm sick of the betrayal. I want
something...better. I want you."

"You have me."

He was quiet a moment, then Ethan said,
"You told me before that you didn't want to give
up your life in NY." He drew in a ragged breath.
His fingers slid down her arm and his hand
caught hers. Held tight. "I can make that happen.
I can make it so that you can stay here. I just need
some time. I can apply the right pressure, I can
make the right deals, and every enemy will go
away."

She actually believed he could do that. She
knew exactly how powerful he truly was. But... "I
think I'd like for us to both start fresh. A clean
slate." They'd both paid enough for the past. "Can
we really do that? Will the FBI let us?"

His smile was grim. "Oh, yeah, baby. They
will. I have something that Agent Monroe wants
very badly. I'll give it to him, and in return, he'll
give us what we need."

Her breath came faster. "Are you really going
to be able to walk away from it all? I know just
how much pull you have in D.C." And leaving that
kind of empire...

"Baby, I'll take plenty of money with me. I'll make sure you always have everything you ever want."

He was all that she wanted. "Ethan—

"And don't worry. You'll still get to contact your step-sister. I guarantee it. You won't lose Julianna. I *can* make that work."

"But everything is about me." Her hair slid over the couch as she shook her head. "What about you? When do you get what *you* want?"

He leaned toward her and pressed a gentle kiss to her lips. "Carly, I already have what I want. Everything I want," he whispered. "And as long as you're with me, that's all I need."

There was so much emotion in his eyes. So much love. Shining right there for her. The rest of the world might look at Ethan and see the big, bad wolf, but she saw the man she loved. The man who hadn't given up on her.

Just as she hadn't given up on him.

And now, it truly was *their* time. "When do we leave?"

He smiled. A drop dead gorgeous grin.

Ethan Barclay. Fucking dangerous and fucking sexy Ethan Barclay.

The man she'd love for the rest of her life.

***

"I'm supposed to let you walk away with a shit-load of cash and *no charges* pending against you?" Victor marched around his office, but the marching was a bit hesitant. Probably due to the still recovering injuries that the agent had.

Bullet wounds could be such a bitch.

"Why the hell..." Victor muttered. "Would I agree to a deal like that? Because I'm an idiot? Because I want to get *demoted* at the Bureau? I mean, yeah, okay, so I was a bit wrong about you and Carly and you weren't the ones killing those guys in New York—"

"Tied Keith and Curtis to those disappearances, didn't you?" But Ethan already knew the truth about those crimes. Carly had told him all, and he'd held her in her hospital bed as she'd cried for those men. Pawns in a deadly game.

Ethan was sick of pawns getting hurt. He was actually sick of so many fucking things. Violence. Death.

He was ready for a better life.

"Yes," Victor gritted out. "We found concrete proof. *In the shrink's own office.* The guy wrote down every detail about the crimes. About how he offered up the victims to Curtis. How Curtis stalked them and killed them." His jaw clenched. "Even how he ditched the bodies."

"Sounds like interesting reading."

"The shrink is a psycho."

"That the clinical term?"

Victor squinted at him. "You trying to be funny? Really? Now? This is the moment you pick?"

Ethan shrugged.

"Dr. Nelson got in with the mob—hell, with *killers*—back when he used to work at Falling Waters State Hospital, a place in upstate New York for criminals deemed...*unstable.* That's when he made his connections and he started bartering secrets. Seems that Nelson had a very unhealthy fascination with the minds of murderers. Over time, he starting selling the secrets he learned." Victor ran his hand over his face. "The jerkoff loved hearing about the brutal crimes, and he sure liked the money he got paid from those bastards."

Ethan paced toward the window. "I'm guessing he'll have plenty of time to talk with killers now." He'll be locked away with them.

"Will he?" Victor demanded.

Ethan looked back at him, making sure his expression appeared all calm and non-threatening.

"Will Dr. Nelson have lots of time to chat? Or will the guy wind up dead within the next few weeks, maybe months? Will someone...*like you*...give an order that he's to be punished for his crimes?"

Again, Ethan shrugged. "I guess that could happen."

"I know you aren't going to confess your plans to me."

Hell, no, he wasn't. Did he look like an idiot?

"But you could still pull strings, right?" Victor pushed. "Or maybe you've already pulled them. Set the guy's death in motion because he hurt *her.*"

Ethan held his gaze. "Do you really think anyone would mourn for Keith Nelson? I'm sure the families of Tage Price, Josh Lavelle, and Ace Patton wouldn't."

"Don't feed me that line. For you, it's not about them. It's about her. What he tried to do to *her*."

Ethan paced toward the agent. "You haven't ever been in love, have you?"

"Fuck, no."

His lips almost twitched. "Love can change a man. Make him less of a monster."

"So you're saying you *aren't* going to kill Nelson?"

No, he wasn't saying that. But he was also thinking that rotting in prison might just be the punishment that drove the doc to the edge. Then over it. *Some people have to suffer first, that way they can truly regret their sins.* "Justice will come around to him, sooner or later. Of that, I have no doubt." And he'd say nothing else. After all, he didn't want to incriminate himself, not when he was still working this deal.

Victor crossed his arms over his chest, but then flinched at the move. Obviously, his wounds still pained him.

Ethan whistled. "I hope you can get back to fighting form soon. Zoe is going to need you."

The faint lines near Victor's eyes deepened. "What do you know?"

"I know Zoe's friend Michelle recently vanished in Vegas...and Zoe rushed back to Sin City in order to save her."

"What?"

"You really need to keep better track of your...assets," Ethan said carefully. After all, if Zoe was tied up with the FBI, then she counted as one of their precious assets, didn't she? "Don't worry. I had a team intercept her. She's currently waiting in a Vegas hotel for you, with twenty-four hour guard service. Those guards will stay there, with her, until they get a call from me saying that *you* are the man who will be taking over her protection."

Ethan knew he was important to the FBI. But Zoe...and her father...they were in a whole different league.

Her father is the freaking devil. And Luther Bates knew where hundreds of skeletons were buried. His work...and the work of some of the most dangerous criminals in the U.S.

And the one piece of leverage that worked to control Bates?

His precious daughter. Zoe.

"Now..." Ethan offered Victor a broad smile. "Since I've saved Zoe's ass...and by association...your ass...let's talk deals again, shall we?" He strode back to the window. "Some place warm. Tropical. I think Carly would look fucking awesome on a beach."

Behind him, Victor growled.

"Don't worry," Ethan added. "When you go to Vegas to collect Zoe, I'll give you the perfect cover. And to thank me for that...I think you'd better make sure my beach has the most beautiful white sand and crystal blue water possible..."

"Sonofabitch."

Ethan knew they had a deal.

***

The breeze blew on Carly's skin as she walked on the beach. A gorgeous, long stretch of beach. And no one else was there. Her toes curled in the white sand and the waves slid forward to meet her, tickling her feet. She laughed and walked deeper into the surf.

"You're beautiful."

Okay, so someone else was there. *He* was there. But Ethan was so much a part of her now...Carly turned toward him, smiling.

He wasn't smiling. His features were tense and so stern and for a second, fear slid through her. *What's happened? What's wrong?*

"Sometimes, I think I should have let you go. I think I shouldn't even touch you." His voice was rough. "But then I know that without you, hell, my life would tear apart."

She offered her hand to him. "I want you to touch me." Him. Always...him.

He wasn't wearing shoes. Just a pair of swim trunks that showed off his six pack abs. They'd only been on the island for a few days. So perfect, she was almost afraid it was all a dream. That she'd wake up...

And he'd be gone.

What if she hadn't found him in that brownstone? What if Curtis had killed him? What if—

"You went back to the past, baby." He took her hand. "You aren't supposed to do that anymore."

She took a quick breath and tasted the salt of the ocean. "You're right. I think it's time I put all of those ghosts to rest."

He nodded, but he was still hesitant. Guarded.

"We're the only ones for miles," she said.

"Yes."

"Good." She pulled her hand from his, and, keeping her eyes on him, Carly stripped. She made sure to toss her clothes farther up on the beach. After all, she didn't want them to float away with the tide.

Ethan's expression hardened even more as he stared at her. Ah, lust. She could see his desire. Just what she wanted. Always. *Ethan...needing me.* "Make love to me?"

"Nothing I want more..." He pulled her close. He kissed her. Deep. Hard. And she kissed him back the same way. But when he started to lift her into his arms, she pushed him away.

"No, *here.*" She bent to the sand. Took a deep breath, then settled down on her back. "Like this."

He was so big and strong as he came down beside her. But he didn't touch her. He almost did, but then his hand fisted.

He knew what she wanted.

They'd been so careful with sex. He'd never been on top of her. Never held her down. Because he hadn't wanted to scare her or bring her ghosts back. But it was time to face those ghosts. With the sun setting, with the waves crashing, with the sand soft beneath her back...this was the place. And Ethan—Ethan was the lover she needed.

So she caught his clenched hand and brought it to her mouth. She kissed his knuckles. "Like this," she said. Then she slid his hand down her body. Over her breasts. Her nipples were already tight. Aching. Eager.

Down, down, she guided his hand. Her legs parted for him. "Like this..." She let his hand go. He was touching her now. Stroking her. Getting her warm and ready for him.

He moved between her thighs, spreading her wider. She reached out to him, but he caught her hands.

Ethan held her hands captive. He stared into her eyes. "Remember...just say *stop*."

Swallowing, she nodded.

Then he let her hands go. He put his fingers on the inside of her thighs. Opened her even wider, and he tasted her. Right there.

Ethan licked and kissed and made her come with a little cry that was lost to the waves.

He moved back up her body. She reached for him once more. This time, he caught her hands in a harder grip. Desire had turned his face harsh.

He put her hands over her head. Caged them with one steely grip around her wrists. Then his gaze came to her face. "Baby?"

"It's you, Ethan. Just you."

He kissed her. She couldn't get enough of him. When he put his cock at the entrance to her body, her hips surged up to meet him. He thrust into her, deep and strong. His body surrounded hers, dominated hers, and he was sliding in and out, fast and deep. The waves were pounding, he was taking her—she was taking *him*.

Her heels dug into the sand as she arched up to meet him. Every hot glide of his body just fed her desire. She was panting and gasping.

"Baby?"

"*Keep...going!*"

And he did. She came with a release that wiped her out. Her heart thundered frantically in her chest, her whole body shuddered as the pleasure blasted her. And he was with her. She felt his release, loved the way he held her even tighter as he drove into her once more. And she loved, *loved* the way he whispered her name.

His fingers caressed her wrist. Slowly, he pushed his body up and stared down at her. "Carly?"

Her lashes lifted. Her heartbeat was still too fast.

"Are you okay?"

She shook her head. "No."

Pain flashed on his face. Pain and fear.

No more of that.

"I'm not okay," she continued as she smiled at him. "I have sand in all kinds of...interesting...places, and I should be running like crazy to wash it all away. Instead all I want...is to make love with you again and again..."

His fear vanished. Pain was replaced by pleasure. Love. Joy.

All of the emotions that she felt, too.

No ghost had come between them. No ghost ever would.

He pressed a tender kiss to her lips. "I know how to take care of the sand..."

"You do? You—" Her words ended in a surprised yelp because he'd moved so fast. He slid out of her and lifted her into his arms. And then he carried her—not back to their beach house, but right out into the water. The waves crashed into them and Ethan just held her tighter.

The sand washed away.

The past washed away.

It was just them.

She wrapped her arms around his neck and knew...yes, this was the man she'd do anything for. She'd trade *anything* for him.

And she also knew—without any doubt whatsoever—that he would do the same for you.

"I love you," Ethan told her.

That was all that mattered.

The End

A NOTE FROM THE AUTHOR

Thank you so much for reading HOLD ON TIGHT! If you enjoyed Jett's story, please consider leaving a review. Reviews help new readers to find great books.

If you'd like to stay updated on my releases and sales, please join my newsletter list.

https://cynthiaeden.com/newsletter/

Again, thank you for reading HOLD ON TIGHT.

Best,
Cynthia Eden
cynthiaeden.com

ABOUT THE AUTHOR

Cynthia Eden is a *New York Times*, *USA Today*, *Digital Book World*, and *IndieReader* best-seller.

Cynthia writes sexy tales of contemporary romance, romantic suspense, and paranormal romance. Since she began writing full-time in 2005, Cynthia has written over one hundred novels and novellas.

Cynthia lives along the Alabama Gulf Coast. She loves romance novels, horror movies, and chocolate.

For More Information

- *https://cynthiaeden.com*
- *http://www.facebook.com/cynthiaedenfanpage*
- *http://www.twitter.com/cynthiaeden*

HER OTHER WORKS

Wilde Ways

- Protecting Piper (Wilde Ways, Book 1)
- Guarding Gwen (Wilde Ways, Book 2)
- Before Ben (Wilde Ways, Book 3)
- The Heart You Break (Wilde Ways, Book 4)
- Fighting For Her (Wilde Ways, Book 5)
- Ghost Of A Chance (Wilde Ways, Book 6)
- Crossing The Line (Wilde Ways, Book 7)
- Counting On Cole (Wilde Ways, Book 8)

Dark Sins

- Don't Trust A Killer (Dark Sins, Book 1)
- Don't Love A Liar (Dark Sins, Book 2)

Lazarus Rising

- Never Let Go (Book One, Lazarus Rising)
- Keep Me Close (Book Two, Lazarus Rising)
- Stay With Me (Book Three, Lazarus Rising)
- Run To Me (Book Four, Lazarus Rising)

- Lie Close To Me (Book Five, Lazarus Rising)
- Hold On Tight (Book Six, Lazarus Rising)
- Lazarus Rising Volume One (Books 1 to 3)
- Lazarus Rising Volume Two (Books 4 to 6)

Dark Obsession Series

- Watch Me (Dark Obsession, Book 1)
- Want Me (Dark Obsession, Book 2)
- Need Me (Dark Obsession, Book 3)
- Beware Of Me (Dark Obsession, Book 4)
- Only For Me (Dark Obsession, Books 1 to 4)

Mine Series

- Mine To Take (Mine, Book 1)
- Mine To Keep (Mine, Book 2)
- Mine To Hold (Mine, Book 3)
- Mine To Crave (Mine, Book 4)
- Mine To Have (Mine, Book 5)
- Mine To Protect (Mine, Book 6)
- Mine Series Box Set Volume 1 (Mine, Books 1-3)
- Mine Series Box Set Volume 2 (Mine, Books 4-6)

Bad Things

- The Devil In Disguise (Bad Things, Book 1)
- On The Prowl (Bad Things, Book 2)

- Undead Or Alive (Bad Things, Book 3)
- Broken Angel (Bad Things, Book 4)
- Heart Of Stone (Bad Things, Book 5)
- Tempted By Fate (Bad Things, Book 6)
- Bad Things Volume One (Books 1 to 3)
- Bad Things Volume Two (Books 4 to 6)
- Bad Things Deluxe Box Set (Books 1 to 6)
- Wicked And Wild (Bad Things, Book 7)
- Saint Or Sinner (Bad Things, Book 8)

Bite Series

- Forbidden Bite (Bite Book 1)
- Mating Bite (Bite Book 2)

Blood and Moonlight Series

- Bite The Dust (Blood and Moonlight, Book 1)
- Better Off Undead (Blood and Moonlight, Book 2)
- Bitter Blood (Blood and Moonlight, Book 3)
- Blood and Moonlight (The Complete Series)

Purgatory Series

- The Wolf Within (Purgatory, Book 1)
- Marked By The Vampire (Purgatory, Book 2)
- Charming The Beast (Purgatory, Book 3)
- Deal with the Devil (Purgatory, Book 4)

- The Beasts Inside (Purgatory, Books 1 to 4)

Bound Series

- Bound By Blood (Bound Book 1)
- Bound In Darkness (Bound Book 2)
- Bound In Sin (Bound Book 3)
- Bound By The Night (Bound Book 4)
- Forever Bound (Bound, Books 1 to 4)
- Bound in Death (Bound Book 5)

Other Romantic Suspense

- One Hot Holiday
- Secret Admirer
- First Taste of Darkness
- Sinful Secrets
- Until Death
- Christmas With A Spy